THIS book is published under the auspices of

THE ULVERSCROFT FOUNDATION

a registered charity in the U.K., No. 264873

The Foundation was established in 1974 to provide funds to help towards research, diagnosis and treatment of eye diseases. Below are a few examples of contributions made by THE ULVERSCROFT FOUNDATION:

* A new Children's Assessment Unit at Moorfield's Hospital, London.

* Twin operating theatres at the Western Ophthalmic Hospital, London.

* A Children's Assessment Unit at Great Ormond Street Hospital for Sick Children, London.

* Eye Laser equipment to various eye hospitals.

If you would like to help further the work of the Foundation by making a donation or leaving a legacy, every contribution, no matter how small, is received with gratitude. Please write for details to:

THE ULVERSCROFT FOUNDATION,
The Green, Bradgate Road, Anstey,
Leicestershire, LE7 7FU, England.

Telephone: (0533) 364325

HUNTED

Not even his twin brother's death had deterred Willmore. Nothing would stop him except a bullet through the head. The Reeses had had bad luck the night Willmore had come along to fight the whole clan. How gun-crazy could a man get? Willmore must be out of his head. But Reese knew a twinge of fear when he thought of the man. What could you do against a man who didn't have the sense to stop coming, against a man who was apparently unafraid of death itself?

MATT CHISHOLM, 1919—

HUNTED

Complete and Unabridged

LINFORD
Leicester

A-1

First Linford Edition
published January 1990

British Library CIP Data

Chisholm, Matt, *1919*–
  Hunted.—Large print ed.—
  Linford western library
  I. Title
  823'.914[F]

  ISBN 0-7089-6798-1

Published by
F. A. Thorpe (Publishing) Ltd.
Anstey, Leicestershire
Set by Rowland Phototypesetting Ltd.
Bury St. Edmunds, Suffolk
Printed and bound in Great Britain by
T. J. Press (Padstow) Ltd., Padstow, Cornwall

1

THE big man on the dun horse sat the saddle, still and tense, listening.

Nothing came out of the night but the after-dark sounds of the brasada, the whirr of insects, the movement of cattle through the thickets.

The fact that he had come this far without running into trouble was a good sign, but he was not an optimist any more. Trouble and Tom Willmore were old friends and expected each other at every turn.

He lifted the lines and the dun stepped off, treading daintily out of the brush onto the prairie that stretched away endlessly into the moonlight. A motte of trees hung like a dark shadow over the plain ahead. The rider hesitated to cross the open space, but it would have added hours to his traveling to have stayed under cover. He drove spurs home and called to the dun. The animal bunched its legs under it and hit a brisk canter. The thud of hoofs on hard ground sounded loudly on the still breathless air.

There was a sound a long way off, it seemed.

Something whined with high-pitched venom past his head. His mind screamed: *I've been shot at.*

No idea where the shot came from, he roweled the horse into a flat run and lay along its distended neck.

There came a staccato mutter of shots and the dun broke its stride, shook its head violently and swerved abruptly to the right. Willmore laid into it with the quirt, but knew he was too late when the animal staggered. It took all his skill as horseman to keep the animal on its feet.

Out of the corner of his eye, he caught sight of a flash from the motte and knew that at least one marksman was hidden there.

The dun slowed, then stopped. It hung its head and coughed.

Willmore knew that he had come to the end of the line.

He gripped the stock of the Spencer, yanked it from the saddle-boot and vaulted from the saddle as the dun went down. The shooting had stopped. He crouched down by the dun and drawing his knife drew it deftly across the animal's throat. A shot would have given him away. Now the light-colored dun was down they couldn't see him too well.

When he had taken his spare ammunition from his wallet behind the saddle, he checked that his revolver was secure in its holster and started crawling toward the nearest brush. He estimated that was a couple of hundred yards away.

Somebody was shouting out there among the trees. He heard the light music of bridle chains and knew that men were mounting up to come looking for him. Urgency touched him. He gave up crawling, reared to his feet and started running.

At once a yell told him that he was spotted and that he had made a mistake.

Too late to rue that. He had to reach the brush as fast as he knew how. His pistoning legs pounded him toward cover as he heard the horses breaking from the timber. He glanced over his shoulder and saw that there were several dark-formed riders coming his way. The brush ahead didn't seem to be getting any nearer.

The thunder of hoofs to his right jerked his head around and brought desperation to him. *There were two bunches of mounted men after him.*

The unaccustomed running labored his breath painfully in his chest. His spine crept as he awaited the shot to hit him in the back.

Then it happened.

A shot came from in front of him.

He had ridden into a complete trap. What the hell now? When you don't know what to do, be still or keep on going. Something plucked at his sleeve. Instinctively, he swerved to the right and found himself in the path of a galloping horse. He levered a round into the breech of the Spencer and fired from the hip as he ran. The rider ducked his head and came on. Willmore stopped running, jacked another round home and fired again. The horse stood on its hind legs whinnying piteously and went over backward. The rider yelled hoarsely.

Willmore went on, running hard for the brush to the right of the hidden guns.

Hoofs pounded near, he dodged the charging horse, saw beast and rider go by and swung the Spencer and fired again. He never knew if he made a hit, but the horseman raced on and was lost in the gloom.

The brush was nearer now.

A man yelled: "There he goes," and there was the hysterical excitement of a huntsman who has sighted his quarry in the voice. He glanced back and saw the line of riders coming from the trees. He ran headlong into the brush and felt the thorns tearing at his flesh and his clothes.

He stumbled and went down. When he reached his feet again, he heard the shouts of the men and the crash of brush as horsemen charged their animals into the undergrowth. There was a horse and rider in front of him, he dodged urgently, but the horse whirled after him. Moonlight glinted on metal and a gun exploded, the horse pounded up to Willmore and he glanced off its shoulder as he dodged again. The horse crashed on into the brush with the rider sawing on the bit to turn it. Willmore darted off in the other direction.

There seemed to be bellowing mounted men all around him. He flung himself flat and started to crawl. He hadn't gone ten yards when a horse almost ran over him. He jumped to his feet to get out of the way, a gun roared almost in his ear and he turned and swung the rifle, firing and levering. The horse reared and the man fell as he tried to get out of the saddle. Willmore ran again, stumbling in his high-heeled cowman's boots. He seemed to run for a long time, then far off in the night he heard the stutter and slam of several rifles.

After that there was utter confusion.

Something knocked a leg from under

him and he was down again. He hit the ground hard and listened to the wind sighing painfully out of his chest. He knew he was hit and something like despair touched him. But he fought his way onto his feet and, hearing the pounding of hoofs behind him, swung around with the Spencer held ready. It was a riderless horse. As it passed close to him, he caught the trailing loose line. The galloping animal nearly tore him from his feet, but as soon as it felt his weight, it halted.

With one leg dead under him, it wasn't an easy task to step into the saddle, but he finally made it, dimly aware that several horsemen were bursting from the brush about a hundred yards away.

The horse he was on lifted at once into a run and after a few jumps his numbed left leg started to send the first threads of agony into his belly. But he could not slow the pace. First he had to stay alive. Second he had to take care of his leg.

When the shouts of the pursuers started becoming louder he knew that he was holding the horse in to favor his leg. He raked home the spurs and gritted his teeth against the pain. He hit a narrow trail and turned along it, heard the men behind come onto it soon after and at once put the pony at the solid wall of the brush. This would find out if the animal was a brush-popper or not.

It was. It went into that brush like a veteran performer and it was as much as Willmore could do to stay in the saddle. Branches and thorns tore at him. His hat was ripped from his head and he would have lost it had it not been for the cord that caught around his neck.

After five minutes of beating his way through the almost impenetrable thickets, he stopped and listened and could hear nothing. That should have given him satisfaction, but it did not. It meant that the men had gone around by the trail to cut him off as he came out on the further trail. He was up the creek without a paddle.

He felt down with his hand, not able to see in the gloom of the brush and found that the saddle carried a rifle-boot and that it was empty. He put the Spencer away and reined the horse around, going quietly back the way he had come.

When he hit the trail again, he found it deserted. He crossed it and slipped into the brush on the further side.

By this time, the full pain of the wounded leg had hit him and he started to feel dizzy. He knew that he was losing a lot of blood and that he would have to stop and fix the wound before long or he'd faint and fall out of the saddle.

By the time he reached the creek, he was bushed. He stepped down from the horse and had to hold onto the saddle horn to stop himself falling. The horse walked on to the water and started drinking. Willmore got down on his belly and drank his fill upstream from the animal. It seemed that he could never drink enough.

Finally, he stopped and sat up. Unstrapping his right chap he rolled it down and found that his levis and the inside of the chap were thick with blood. There was no time for niceties. Tearing a strip from the tail of his shirt, he made it into a tight wad and pressed it on the wound, then he strapped it loosely to his leg with his bandanna, found a short stick and twisted the tourniquet tight. The throbbing stopped.

He wondered if there was any lead in there and thought that most likely there was. The fear of losing his leg touched him and he shuddered. A terrible fate for a horseman. There would be no future— not that there was much likelihood of one as things were.

After nerving himself to stand on the leg again, he heaved himself wearily to his feet, thinking of his crazy night's work, his shooting of Jet Reese, his flight. He had been out of his head with defeat and rage. Now he had finished himself. The Reeses and the countryside that listened to them and paid them homage would be out after him. He was fair game to any man with a gun.

He limped to the horse. Walking was

like dragging a leg with an iron ball chained to it. He clung to the saddle, taking his weight off his feet and heaving himself up so that he could get his sound foot into the stirrup-iron. Dragging the injured leg over the cantle gave him some trouble. After three attempts, he made it, nearly fainting in the process. Once in the saddle, he sat motionless, trying to pull himself together, ears and eyes alert as he could make them, listening to the sounds of the brush. From far off, thunder rumbled.

Rain, he wondered. *Could there possibly be rain? That might save me.*

But what should he do? They would expect him to go home. There was nothing there for him any more.

The thunder rolled again.

He must have nodded off. There was a crash behind him in the brush, the horse under him stirred and whinnied. He came to himself with a start and a flutter of panic, his hand searching fumblingly for the butt of his belt-gun.

A man shouted.

He grabbed the line and made up his mind to make a dash through the creek.

A rifle slammed flatly.

Something thudded into the saddle horn and he felt the reverberations of the hit through his whole body. The horse jumped. Another rifle went off and something struck him sharply on the crown of his head knocking him forward onto the neck of the horse. After that his actions were involuntary. He raked the belly of the animal with his spurs and felt it leap forward under him. His arms clasped the muscled neck. The creek splashed around him. He knew the horse was in a panic and would run hard when it reached the further bank.

2

HE was lying on his back.

He squinted upward. Above him through an opening in the brush, he saw the gray lowering mass of rain cloud. The rain fell heavily, beating on his face. When he slowly raised his hands from the ground they were covered in brown mud. Rain and red dust combined. The rare rain had come to the Red Creek country of Texas and it was now awash.

He tried to move his leg and heard himself groan. He forced himself to sit up and found that his head ached so unbearably that for a moment he shut his eyes against the pain.

When he ran a hand through his hair, he winced and withdrew a hand covered in blood. He knew then that he had been creased. Looking around warily he saw that there was no horse in sight. The animal had sensibly gone home.

He knew there had been a horse, he told himself over and over, yet he couldn't remember what horse. What was its color? No answer came.

His attempt to stand up was pathetic. Not being able to rise in a forward position, he rolled over, got himself on hands and knees and got up that way. His wounded leg felt dead. He viewed the bandanna wound around it with some astonishment and realized with a paralyzing shock that he could not remember being injured, nor of tying the tourniquet around it.

My God, he thought in a panic, *what happened to me?*

He bent and with stiffened fingers loosened the tight cloth, feeling the blood throbbing into the wound at once. When the blood had soaked into bandanna, he twisted the stick again and tied it firm. Slowly it came to him that he needed help desperately and he needed it fast.

Looking about him, battling to stay on

his feet, fighting the dizziness that fought to overpower him, he saw that he was standing on a trail. It was not wide, no more than twenty feet across and was grown on either hand with dense scrub oak. Familiar country at least.

Which way to go?

Anyway might be the right way, anyway the wrong. Maybe any road at all was wrong. Whichever way he turned he might walk into the men who had put the bullet in his leg and had creased him.

So choose.

He turned left and walked.

It was killing work and every now and then he stopped and rested, mostly when he had fallen down. The trail was thick mud under his boots and his tread was unsteady. Whenever he put any weight on his wounded leg it threatened to give under him and it slipped easily. It did not take much time to convince him that he couldn't go on much longer. He was dazed and he couldn't think. He tried to recollect the events that had taken place before he lost consciousness, but failed.

He tried to think about himself, what his circumstances were, but he failed. Then he asked himself, the simple question as he lay face downward in the mud: *Who am I?* And could not answer that either. He was so weak that he wanted to weep, but some remaining pride prevented that.

Finally, he passed out again.

He came vaguely to himself for a brief moment, wrenched from unconsciousness by acute pain as his leg and his head were jolted. He heard himself cry out, then lay still, trying to find out what was happening to him.

The sounds and the jolting told him that he was in a wagon of some sort.

Dim panic came again and he thought: *They've got me. They've got me.*

But he didn't know who *they* were any more than he knew who *he* was. He didn't know anything about anything but the pain that hammered and swooped through his enfeebled body.

He wondered where they were taking

him . . . He floated off on a blood-red sea of pain and delirium.

There was no knowing where he was. He knew only that he was warm and dry, that he lay enjoying a heady drowsiness. A light showed faintly. It was a long time before he summoned either enough interest or strength to lift his head and to look around.

Before he did that, he became aware of a dull ache in the region of his thigh, but it did not trouble him overly and he lay for some time content to hover between sleep and wakefulness. Finally, after unrecorded time, he heard a faint sound near him and lifted his head to find its origin.

He saw at once that he was in a large room that looked as though it were part of a shack. There was dried mud in the chinks of the hewn logs and oiled paper at the windows and the glow of a stove in the far corner.

Slowly it came to him that for the moment he was safe. He was, he now saw, lying in a comfortable bed between white sheets and under his head was a soft down pillow. He was in the hands of someone who at least had not shown that they wished him harm.

He tried to raise his head some more to discover if he could see his gun near, but the light in the place was so poor he could make out few details. A faint lamp burned at the other end of the place and in the other circle of its light he made out a human form. At first he could not make out if it were a man or a woman, but when it moved and stood up he saw that it was a woman. Tall, high-breasted and fair-haired.

He tried to lift himself with an elbow and failed. He lay shaking on the bed, knowing how weak he was. Turning his head, he said softly:

"Ma'am."

He must have no more than whispered, for she did not hear. He tried again.

"Ma'am."

He was astonished at the hoarse croak that came from his lips. She heard him and, turning, picked up the lamp and came toward him.

The brightness of the light hurt his eyes, but he did not take them from the woman. Maybe he was pretty sick, but he wasn't so sick that he couldn't tell a fine-looking woman when he saw one. Her easy movement spoke of physical strength; her direct gaze of honesty. The down-turned corners of her well-shaped and generous mouth told of bitterness. Yet he couldn't remember when he had taken to a woman in so brief a time. He looked at her and there that feeling was.

Something seemed to click in his brain, to click on blankness and dark. What could he remember?

She was standing close to the bed, holding the light high so that she could see him the better. Their eyes met.

"So," she said in a soft deep voice, "you decided to wake up?"

He tried to smile, but his face felt stiff and cracked. He put his hand to his cheek and found many days of beard-growth there. How long had he been here in this bed?

"Can you tell me where I'm at, ma'am?"

She showed faint surprise.

"Don't tell me you don't know the Widow Craytham?" she said.

He frowned, trying to remember. Was that a name he should know? He remembered nothing and again that slow fear ebbed through him, the fear of a man living timelessly and without identity.

"The Widow Craytham," he said musingly to himself. "Is that you, ma'am?" She nodded. "Should I know you?"

"I should of thought," she said, "that most everybody knew me." He didn't miss the bitterness in her voice.

He lay still, thinking. It was hard work driving his battered brains. There was a curious sensation about his head as though a bee buzzed in it. Not exactly pain, but akin to it. He put a tentative hand up to his head and found the bandage that went right over the top. When he touched it felt very sore.

"They creased you," she told him, folding her arms over her proud breasts, "and they shot you in the right leg." She made the statement flatly, as if a man could get himself hit in two places with lead any day of the week.

"Who's *they*, ma'am?" he asked.

"How should I know? How come you don't know?"

The question defeated him utterly. He waved a hand helplessly. The movement brought a slight throbbing from his head. He searched his mind for memories, for the very words he wanted to speak.

"I reckon I don't remember a thing," he said. "Sounds kind of foolish. Not even my name."

Her eyes were wide. Fine dark eyes.

"It must be the creasing," she said. "I've heard of such a thing. Your memory'll come back when you're stronger."

"Not even my name," he said

They stayed very still, not even looking at each other.

"How long," he asked, "have I been here?"

"A week."

And the men who had shot him might still be looking for him. But they hadn't found him yet, so he could be in a pretty safe place.

"Do you know me, ma'am?"

She nodded. "I seen you around."

"Where?"

"In town. Boone."

"My name?"

"Willmore. Tom Willmore."

It didn't mean a thing to him. It could have been the name of a stranger.

"I've been a lot of trouble, I reckon."

"Forget it."

"No, ma'am. I shan't forget it. Can you make a guess who shot me?"

"Maybe."

"Try."

"One of the Reeses."

"Why should one of these Reeses want me dead?"

"They killed your brother."

His brother!

The fearful sensation of being lost and unidentifiable came over him again. He knew of no brother. Could the woman be conning him? What possible reason could she have? He looked back at her. Those eyes were honest. They looked directly into his, unwaveringly.

"So," he said, "I went after the Reeses and they shot me."

"It could have been like that," she said.

He was very tired suddenly and his eyes became heavy. Thinking about his problem, he fell asleep, suddenly.

3

HE sat on the edge of the stoop's shadow, warm and comfortable in the sun, soaking in the heat and feeling that every minute in it increased his strength by a fraction. He had his pipe going and for a moment knew utter contentment. Not a dozen yards away the woman was busy at her wash tub. He admired her movements that were made with the certainty of a man.

A hundred yards or so away, the two boys Bobby and Jimmy roped and rode the sorrel colt. Every now and then it threw them, playfully and without disaster, and he could hear their excited yells. They were good kids. They lacked a man's hand and they had received that when after a few days of being out of bed Willmore had caught them sassing their mother. His heavy hand had brought a sudden wish for politeness to the family.

Tom Willmore limped away from the house, favoring his injured leg, bearing down heavily on his crutches. He walked down the brasada trail, little more than a path and, though his memory for details may have failed him, he knew that he was at home here. Memory of the past he might not have, but at once the names of the brush and growths he saw about him came to him. Here was the dense low black chaparral, there the dense mesquite and its nourishing beans; there was the prickly catclaw, *guajilla*, and there the *huisache*, no longer golden flowered as in the spring. And then, as he came to a draw, was a close mass of bee brush and there solitary and wicked was the accursed *jonco*. This was the countryside that was hell on men and horses and worse for women. Yet a country that he loved and was in his blood.

He stopped every now and then, looking about him, savoring it, even the blasting heat. The sweat ran from under his hat band, it ran down his body and soaked his shirt. The brush was a thorny

25

impenetrable oven, but it was home to him and he knew it without a doubt.

Something stirred uneasily in the brush near at hand and he reckoned it was a wild-as-deer longhorn alarmed at his approach. It had taken up its daytime hiding place in the brush and would come out at night to feed on the grass of the prairies.

And suddenly, Willmore came on one of these prairies, a great glade of grass, surrounded by ever encroaching chaparral.

Here he sat and rested a while in the shade of a spreading oak until he felt his strength come back to him and then rose and notched the bark so that a blaze showed. He hobbled off thirty yards and dropped one of his crutches in the dust.

Now came the moment of assessment.

Just how good was he with a gun?

He looked at the target he had cut and saw it showing faintly in the blue-black shadow of the oak. He knew that shooting from sunlight into shadow could be tricky. There was some knowledge from the past. The target was not as big as a man's hand, no bigger than his heart. Surely he had chosen a most difficult shot.

Slowly he lifted the old Remington from leather and inspected it. The old converted cap-and-ball. Maybe some men would sneer at it, but it felt just right in his hand.

Taking his weight from his right leg and leaning heavily on the crutch he lifted the gun to eye-level and sighted carefully.

He didn't fire.

The deliberate action felt wrong. He returned the gun to its holster and stared at the target.

He stood waiting, growing strangely at peace with the world, relaxed, and knew that he had done this many times before. Almost without his knowing it, following nothing but trained instinct, his right hand slid effortlessly to the butt of the gun, pulled it in one smooth movement from leather and continued that movement until the gun came up in line with the target. Almost without knowing it, he willed his thumb to cock the hammer and his forefinger to squeeze the trigger. It all just happened. The gun roared and he heard the bullet strike home. Then, because he had crouched in some forgotten habit as the gun came up, he lost his balance and fell.

The fall hurt his leg like hell, but it struck him as funny and he laughed, which surprised him, because until that moment he didn't seem to know that he was a laughing man.

He just lay there in the grass and dust and laughed and it was like a magical release.

Gathering his crutches, he put the gun away after wiping the dust from it and reared to his feet, going hobbling and swinging to look at the target.

When he reached it, he saw that, without consciously aiming, he had hit the heart-sized mark dead center.

That brought sober thought.

Either he had had the luck of the devil or he was good with a gun.

He took the crutch from his right

armpit and holding it in his left hand repeated that draw again and again. There seemed no doubt about that part of the operation.

He was handy with a gun all right.

And somehow without any reason he was thinking about that unknown brother of his, the brother the woman had told him about. He wondered what kind of a man he had been this younger brother. Gay? Tough? Dependable? The pain of trying to remember his only kin was suddenly almost unbearable. He stood there a long while, motionless.

His heart leapt in alarm when a voice said behind him—

"Take your hand from your gun."

His spine went cold.

Had it happened so soon? Had his unknown enemies caught up with him already? He wanted to tear himself around and look at the man's face, to know if he recognized him, if it brought back any memory. Surely if the hate was deep enough . . .

He didn't move.

Trained caution took command. The coldness went from him and he found himself relaxed just as he had been before he drew the gun back there.

"Who is this?" he asked in a neutral tone.

"Turn around slow," the man said, "an' let me see your face."

Slowly, awkwardly on the one crutch, Willmore turned.

A man stood a dozen yards away and the handsome face meant nothing to him. He looked at the weather-beaten lines, the mustache, the cold gray eyes and could remember nothing. But the man knew him, the recognition showed at once in his eyes.

"So it *is* you, Willmore," he said.

Willmore was at a loss.

"It's me," he said. "What's the gun for?"

There was something of the dandy about the man. There were silver conchos on the gun-barrel chaps, silver on his gun-belt. The bandanna was new and of pure silk.

"You've got the nerve," the man said almost admiringly. He spoke without anger. "You murderin' coyote, it's to kill you with."

Willmore waited calmly, not speaking, knowing what he was going to do.

He was going to kill this man. He was going to draw under the muzzle of that ready gun and kill its owner.

And the decision didn't surprise him. He knew that he could do it.

Coldly, he watched the man raise his gun till it was sighted dead center on his heart. Peace flowed over Willmore. His brain commanded his hand. He stood relaxed and at ease. He watched the man's thumb brace against the hammer, unsuspecting Willmore's impossible intent.

Willmore's right hand swept his gun from leather.

They both seemed to fire in the same instant.

The man was jerked backward and around as if he were a giant puppet on a string. One arm flung out sideways and his gun fell from nerveless fingers. As he started to go down, Willmore automatically cocked and fired a second time.

The man hit dirt and a small cloud of dust arose.

Willmore put his gun away, picked up the crutch he had dropped and swung toward the body. When he stopped and looked down, he saw that he had shot him first through the heart and then through the head. That was the professional's *coup de grace*. He knew that this was not the first time he had done this. Yet there was deep regret in him. The taking of life did not lie lightly on him.

He thought. This man had come here to kill him. He had known him. Was he then one of these Reeses whom Willmore and his brother had been up against, one of the men who had killed his brother? He looked at the now ashen face with the neat bullet hole between the eyes and knew that he might be looking at the face of the man who killed that unknown brother.

Turning, he swung himself on the crutches back to the trail and went stolidly back to the house. There was some reluctance on his part, a natural squeamishness. He had killed a man and was preparing to face a respectable woman.

She and her two boys were waiting in the yard, watching him approach.

When he came up to them, he asked somberly: "Did you hear the shots?"

"We heard them." He looked her in the face and saw that she was pale. Her eyes were dark and burning. She looked so over-powered by some strong emotion that he thought she was going to faint. She turned to the boys. "Go find something to do, boys," she said. "I have to talk with Mr. Willmore."

"Aw, ma . . ."

"Go ahead now. Go down to the south pasture and see if you can put a rope on that sorrel colt again and bring him here for me."

They liked the idea of that. Yeah, they cried, they'd do it. They ran off to the shed and collected ropes, scurrying off across the yard, excited. The man and the woman stood wordlessly, watching them go.

"That man—," Willmore began, watching them disappearing down the brasada trail. A gasp from the woman brought his head around to her sharply. She was gazing at him hard, trying to read something in his eyes.

"He came to kill you," she said in a whisper.

"You knew?"

She nodded. "I knew."

"Did he tell you?"

"He didn't say anything. But I knew. And there wasn't anything I could do about it. You have to believe that." She was vehement.

"Sure, I believe it. What could you have done?"

"What. . . ? Did you. . . ?" One slender hand was at her mouth now. She was scared.

"I killed him," he said flatly. "I had to. He held a gun on me and told me he was goin' to kill me." He smiled wryly. "I didn't know him from Adam. Did you?"

"Yes," she said and she choked on the word.

"Who was he?" he said.

"He was my husband."

Willmore didn't know what to do or say. There was a terrible silence between them.

Finally, he said: "Ma'am . . ." He couldn't find the words. "I didn't know."

Her voice was broken. "How could you know? He would . . . have killed . . . you."

They looked at each other, mute in their misery and he was surprised that he knew that there was no hate between them. The tears started in her eyes, her mouth trembled and suddenly she was in his arms, weeping. He lost his balance a little and leaned back against the upright of the stoop for support. Standing there, holding her, he let her cry herself out.

At last she released herself and went wooden-faced to a chair by the house-door and sat down. She waved a hand to another chair, a rocker, near it.

"Sit down," she said. "I think we should talk."

He swung once on the crutches, turned with some skill and dropped heavily into the rocker.

"You don't have to tell me anything you don't want to," he said.

"I don't *have* to tell you anything at all," she told him. "I want to. Tom, I just have to get this off my chest. I kept it tight here inside me too long."

He noted the use of his first name. He liked it. He knew that she had been scarcely aware of using it. Things were like that suddenly between them without any warning. There was her husband lying dead out there on the prairie and already she was close to Willmore. She gave him that direct look of hers.

"I knew who you were the moment I saw you, when I picked you up on the road. I knew Bob, my husband, wanted you dead. I knew it and I kept you here, hoping, praying he wouldn't come back yet. When he came I didn't expect him. I know I did wrong. It might be you who

36

was killed. But you have to understand. There hasn't been . . . anyone, for a long time. Nigh on a couple of years Bob has been like a stranger to me. Away weeks at a time, sometimes months, God knows where. Over the Border, up to Denver. He didn't want the boys or me. I never know why he didn't ride out and never come backa-tall."

"The boys," he asked, "how're they goin' to take this?"

"He's a stranger to them. He was either hard with them or ignored them. Maybe they'll guess, but we must never tell them you killed Bob."

"All right," he said. "Did your husband ride with the Reeses?"

She shot him a quick look.

"You catch on," she said. "Yes, he rode with them. He did gun chores for them. When you killed him, you paid a debt for mankind, I reckon. It's a hard thing to say, but it's true."

"But you cried over him," he said gently.

Again that direct look.

37

"I loved him once. I guess I cried for all the wasted years, living out here on next to nothing with the two boys. What chance have they?"

"Every chance," he said. "They have a fine woman for a mother."

He stood up as quickly as he could on his wounded leg because it embarrassed him to say that.

"Now," she said, "we have to get you away from here."

"You were in no hurry before this."

"The Reeses will know. They know Bob came home. Somebody'll come looking for him. You must try sitting a horse."

He turned and faced her, leaning against the stoop rail, looking down at her upturned face from his great height.

"Who do I know in this country?" he asked. "Who is there I can rely on?"

"I don't know. I didn't know you well enough to say who you could trust. There's your uncle, of course."

Was there faint derision in her voice?

"Who's he?"

"Charlie Willmore."

"Cattleman?"

"No. County sheriff."

That shook him.

"Wait a minute," he said. "You told me the Reeses killed my brother." She nodded. "Surely if this Charlie Willmore's the sheriff—"

"What could he do against the Reeses? What could anybody do? Except you?"

"Me?"

She rose from the chair and stood facing him.

"Why do you think they shot Bart?"

"Bart?"

"Your brother." So his brother's name was Bart."

"Why did they shoot him?"

"He went after them and they thought he was you."

"Why should they think that?"

She waved her hands at the impossibility of the task of filling his vacant memory for him.

"I'm not doing this very well, am I?

You were both deputy-sheriffs. You were both alike."

The news stunned him.

"Why don't I have a badge on my vest now?"

"You resigned when they killed Bart. Talk was that your uncle would not or could not do anything about it."

"How alike were we?"

"Alike as two peas in a pod."

"Twins?"

"Yes."

"How alike were we really. Could you tell the difference between us?"

"Yes, I could."

"How?"

"There was a wildness about Bart. You were steadier. Oh, Bart was nice all right. They didn't come any nicer than Bart."

"Did you know him well?" There was no offence in the question.

"Not well. But everybody knew Bart. He got around. Got to know people. They said one day he'd get to be sheriff, people thought so much of him."

"Except the Reeses."

"That's right."

He hobbled down from the stoop and started toward the shed.

"Where're you going?" the woman asked.

He stopped and said: "You stay here and keep the boys near when they get back," and she knew that he was going to bury the dead man. Her husband. As he went into the shed to fetch out the spade she turned into the house to cut off the sight of him going to bury her past. She busied herself at the stove, not wanting to think, not wanting to remember. She felt that she should be more sorry, but she was an honest woman and knew that with her husband's death she had been relieved of a great weight. Now she really was a widow; it was no longer a term of derision.

A short while after, the boys came in with their two ropes on the sorrel colt. They didn't need them both, for the young animal grew quiet as soon as it felt a rope on its neck. It was going to prove a gentle saddle-horse. Strange in so young a horse. She had it in mind that Tom Willmore could ride it.

4

THE boys tied the animal to the stoop rail and she said: "Get a saddle and bridle on it, boys." There was only her husband's saddle and she felt bad about Willmore having to use that. She told herself that she should not be so sensitive. This was the frontier and there was no room for softness.

Laughing and fighting amiably together, the boys got the saddle and bridle on the horse and the woman said to the elder: "Bob, you get in that saddle and take the kinks out of that animal. Mr. Willmore has to ride it and we don't want him having trouble with that wounded leg, do we?"

Bob untied the sorrel and stepped up into the saddle. She watched him with pride as he did so. He was a fine horseman already.

The young horse whirled away from the

stoop and pitched its way across the yard. Bob held the lines high and raised his right hand to show that he wasn't touching leather. He yipped a couple of times to excite the colt, but after a half-dozen pitches the sorrel had shown its independence and quietened down.

Willmore appeared on the edge of the yard. He looked pale, but he was grinning.

"Well ridden, kid," he said.

The boy sat the saddle, patting the sorrel's shoulder, glowing.

Jimmy yelled: "He ain't the on'y one, Mr. Willmore. I kin ride the kinks outa any hoss."

"Isn't not ain't," said his mother automatically.

Bob brought the sorrel to the stoop and dismounted. Willmore put the spade away in the shed and swung himself on his crutches to the colt, handed them to Jimmy and got aboard. It felt good to be in the saddle again. He trotted the animal around the yard and found that riding brought twinges to his leg, but not nearly so bad as he had thought it would.

5

ANY stranger seeing them ride along the brush country trail would have thought them husband and wife and two sons. Willmore thought that it was as though the dead man had never existed. The husband lay in his lonely brasada grave and the wife rode into town with another man. And what else, Willmore asked himself, would he have had her do? He owed her everything and that included his life. He glanced at her and she met his glance unwaveringly, but he saw with some relief that she was taking this hard. The man's death had shaken her and she was holding on tight. He gave her a smile and the one she gave back wavered uncertainly.

The boys, all unaware, were excited at going into town. They raced their horses in the heat until Willmore had to stop them, telling them that was no way to treat horseflesh and they sat their saddles and listened to him wide-eyed. They accepted him as their authority and this was not lost on the woman.

When an hour before noon they neared the town nervousness fell on Willmore. Here he would be face to face with a past that he did not know. The face of every man who knew him would be that of a stranger.

They came first to a scattering of Mexican *jacals*, flimsy, makeshift habitations of a poor people with a goat-pen maybe on the side of the house or a few hens pecking in the dust around the door. The people watched them out of their dark withdrawn eyes. One man, sitting at his door, arose and lifted a hand in salute.

"Don Thomás."

A quick showing of white teeth in a dark face.

Willmore responded, wondering: "Have I friends then among the Mexicans?"

"Who was that?" he asked the woman

when they had passed and she said: "Miguel Ortega."

"Ever seen me speakin' with him?"

"No."

The jacals gave way to more substantial adobes. Here were burros and people on the rough street, traders, sweetmeat vendors. Their horses had to edge their way in places through the crowd and Willmore was confused by the profusion of color, sights and smells.

Another man lifted a hand and flashed a smile.

"Don Tomás."

Willmore heard himself speaking in Spanish, asking after the man who greeted him and then they came to the bridge and the trees on the creekside and there on the other side of the water was the Anglo town. Their hoofs thudded hollowly on the bridge timbers and a moment later they were treading the dust of the street. Here, though the adobe still persisted, houses made of lumber and brick appear from a frontier village. A ranch buckboard clattered by driven by

48

an ageing cowhand who gave Willmore a
startled glance as he drove by.

Willmore looked at the signs. The
Lucky Chance Saloon. Hardecker's
Emporium. A blacksmith's. The Mulland
County Bank. Sheriff's office.

He turned and looked at the woman
and saw that she was watching him. The
boys were heading for a hitch-rail, piling
from their saddles and tying their
animals. Willmore and the woman reined
in beside them and he helped her from
the saddle. A buggy went by driven by
a middle-aged woman who stared. Other
people were staring at Willmore and the
woman. He felt stiff and embarrassed,
wondering how many people whom he
knew he had ignored.

A tall man had come to the door of the
sheriff's office. He wore a gray shirt and
a leather vest with a star on it. His hair
and mustache were white against the deep
brown of his face. Store-bought pants
were tucked into knee-high boots that
sported their mule-ears on the outside. He
didn't wear a gun. He was staring hard

at Willmore and when he saw Willmore looking his way he lifted a tentative hand.

"Your uncle," the woman said.

"Excuse me a moment, ma'am," Willmore said. "I reckon I'll go talk with him."

"Go ahead," she said, stepping up onto the sidewalk. "I'll be in the store with the boys."

He started away from her, but was brought to a startled halt by a young woman who was suddenly in his path.

In that first moment of assessment he saw an extremely pretty girl of no more than twenty, dressed in gingham and bonnet, basket on her arm. Her skin was tanned, her hair dark and her eyes of the deepest violet. She was small and neat and in her eyes were recognition and a harrowing anxiety. At once Willmore realized in some panic that here was someone he knew well.

"Tom," she cried out and was in his arms with her head pressed against his shoulder. He held her to him instinctively and glanced around. Mrs. Craytham was watching. She looked startled and un-decided.

"My God," the girl was saying, pulling back her head and showing that there were tears in her eyes. "I thought you were dead."

"No," he said. "They hit me in the leg is all."

"Why didn't you let me know? It's been two weeks. I've been beside myself. First Bart . . . now you."

Her voice broke when she mentioned Bart's name.

Willmore wondered to whom she belonged, him or Bart.

"Listen," he said. People had stopped on both sides of the street and were watching them with open curiosity. "They did something else to me." She looked startled. "They shot me in the head. Creased me." He looked at her closely, holding her by both arms away from him, wondering if she would be able to accept the truth and not make a scene. She fixed her eyes on his, still wondering. "They shot away my memory, I reckon. I don't remember a thing. Nothing. I don't know who you are."

"You what?"

"I don't know who you are," he repeated in a low voice.

She didn't say anything, but gazed at him in incredulity. He wished to heaven they were out of sight of all these people. Out of the corner of his eye he caught sight of a movement and looking to his left he saw that the sheriff was walking toward them.

"Let's go into the sheriff's office," he said. "We can talk there."

Gripping her by one arm and limping badly he started her across the street and met the sheriff in the center. The sheriff repeated the girl's words.

"My God, Tom," he said, "I thought you were dead."

Another rapid assessment to be made.

This man was old, but he was no weakling. He held himself straightened and was honed down to bone and rawhide. From what Mrs. Craytham had told him he had made up his mind that his uncle was a coward. But he would bet this man was no coward. Shrewd and careful more like.

Willmore gave the older man a wry grin.

"Almost but not quite," he said. He hesitated. "Er—there are complications. We should talk. How about going into your office?"

The old man gave him a long look and said: "Sure. Come on."

He led the way back across the street with Willmore and the girl behind him.

In the office, after they had pushed their way through the curious people on the sidewalk, Willmore closed the door and faced them. The girl spoke first.

"I can't believe it, Tom. I just can't," she said.

"Can't believe what?" the sheriff asked.

"He says that he's lost his memory."

The sheriff swung his blue-eyed gaze back to his nephew. He didn't say a word for a moment.

Finally, he asked: "Is this true, Tom?"

Willmore took off his hat and bent his

head. Mrs. Craytham had removed the bandage that morning. He fingered the top of his scalp gingerly.

"They creased me with a .30-30," he said. "I reckon they busted either my skull or something in my head. I half-woke up on the trail and didn't remember a thing. All I knew was that men were after me because I'd been shot. Mrs. Craytham found me on the trail, toted me home in her wagon. I'd be dead if it wasn't for her." He thought that the girl sniffed and that annoyed him. "All I know about myself is what she's told me."

The sheriff gave him another piercing look, turned, walked to his desk and sat down behind it.

"If this don't beat the band," he said. "Look, do you know who I am?"

"You're my uncle and you're the sheriff. Bart an' me served under you as deputies."

"You know Bart's dead, boy?"

"Yes."

"Who's this young lady?"

54

Willmore shook his head. "I don't know," he said.

The girl gave a little sob.

My God, thought Willmore, *does that mean she's my girl?*

"This is Mary and she was Bart's wife."

Willmore looked at her, trying to picture her as his sister-in-law. She looked more like a kid sister. So this was the woman who had loved and wept for Bart, the unknown brother.

"You say Mrs. Craytham cared for you?" the sheriff asked.

Willmore nodded. "I reckon she saved my life."

Speculatively, Charlie Willmore said: "Craytham's wife. Don't that beat the band. You see Craytham?"

"Yes."

Something that Willmore could not measure came into his uncle's eyes. He could tell if it were surprise or fright.

"More to the point," the elder man said, "did Craytham see you?"

"Good enough to hold a gun on me."

There was a silence during which the sheriff sat staring in what looked like plain stupidity at his nephew.

"Did Reese send him?" he asked at last.

"It didn't make much difference whether Reese or the devil himself sent him. He came to kill me."

"How do you know?"

"He told me so."

The sheriff was on his feet. There was no doubt that he was alarmed. "What did he do? Where'd he go?"

"I killed him."

The sheriff was so profoundly shaken that he blasphemed in front of a woman.

"Jesus!" He turned to the girl. "You'd best go, Mary, my dear. Tom an' me have to talk."

She came toward Willmore and put a hand on his arm.

"Come and see me when you and uncle have talked."

"I'll do that," he told her and she

walked out onto the sidewalk, pushing her way through the people there.

Uncle and nephew looked at each other.

"I just don't know what to say," the elder man said. "Care for a drink?"

"No, thank you."

"Some things maybe I should ought to tell you, Tom."

"Such as?"

"Like you haven't behaved well over what the Reeses did."

"Killing my brother?"

The sheriff waved his hands helplessly. "Hell," he said. "Ask yourself—what else could they do. My God, he went out there with blood in his eye. He was goin' to commit murder!"

"Why?"

The sheriff went to reply, but was interrupted.

A sound came from behind Willmore. He turned and found Mary Willmore standing in the open doorway. She looked alarmed.

"Tom," she said, "the Reeses're in town."

The sheriff came forward and put a hand on his arm. not taking his eyes from his face. "No trouble, now, son," he said.

"Ride out, for God's sake," the girl said. Then as he stood immobile, she pleaded. "Please."

"All right," he said.

"Quick, they're mounted and they're headed this way."

He shook off his uncle's restraining hand. As he reached the door, the girl stood aside and there stepping up onto the sidewalk was Mrs. Craytham.

"The Reeses," she said the moment she caught sight of him. He saw the two boys standing on the street, looking first at him and then along the street. He gave Mary a little smile and started across the street toward his horse saying to Mrs. Craytham. "I'll pick you up on the way back to your place, ma'am."

Reaching his horse, he swung awkwardly into the saddle and wheeled the animal around. He glanced back and saw several horsemen coming around the far corner a couple of hundred yards away. He touched the sorrel with the spurs and sent it down the street at a trot. He felt humiliated and knew that it was not in his nature to run. With a confusion of thought and puzzlements, he clattered across the bridge, went out through the Mexican houses and was soon in the brush.

He went along the main trail for a half-mile then swung off it onto a shoulder of brush-strewn hill, got into the chaparral and waited.

There was no need to wait long. Within five minutes he heard the sounds of several approaching horsemen. Dismounting, he held the sorrel's nose and waited.

There were half-a-dozen of them, all big men mounted on breedy-looking horses, better stock than could be raised on the grass of Texas.

The man in the lead was not the leader, but a bulky cowman mounted on a lively bay. Foam flecked the animal's chest and shoulders as the powerful rider held it in against its fiery will. The man was gross, unshaven, mean-eyed and shouted his conversation over his shoulder to the men behind him in a hoarse baritone. Willmore didn't catch the words, but the men behind evidently thought they were amusing. The next man was big, but was finely proportioned. His features were good, his chin shaven and his heavy fair mustache neatly trimmed. His clothing was that of a working cowman: leather vest, blue woollen shirt, levis covered by shotgun chaps.

The next man, though insignificant in size, though sitting his saddle poorly, was without doubt the leader. Willmore never knew how he knew, but there was no doubt in his mind. There was an air of confidence and command about the man that was evidence enough. This man looked dwarfed by the others, he looked alien to them, yet his features showed that he belonged to the same breed. He was bearded fairly and his skin showed a curiously pale transparency in a land where flesh was leathern and weather-beaten. The hands were as pale and shapely as a woman's. The clothes were good from the white shirt, the prince albert coat down to the gray pants tucked into hand-tooled boots.

Willmore thought that the thin man behind him was also a Reese. He had the same patrician nose as the other three, the same air of owning the world. But the two men who brought up the rear told the world that they were hired hands. Whether they were simply cowhands was another matter. There was an air of hard competence about them that spoke of something more. Willmore thought that they would prove skillful with the revolvers that they wore at their hips. In fact, every man there looked as though he were a man not to be argued with. They were all armed with revolvers and saddleguns.

Willmore waited patiently until the sound of their going had died and their faint dust was teasing at his nostrils. Then he mounted the sorrel and faced the fact that he might be a stranger in this country, he knew so little about. He was stuck between the Craytham place and the town. Everywhere else was foreign territory to him.

6

THERE was one thought and one thought only that filled the horizon of Willmore's mind: how to survive.

In that past beyond the barrier of his memory, he must have been a wary man. Now he sat outside Mrs. Craytham's barn, smoking the pipe that he had found in his pocket in the cool of the dusk, and thinking. Through the lighted window of the house he could see the woman moving about. Of the people he had seen in the day past, she seemed the most likely that he could trust, but even with her he could not be sure. He had killed her husband. He had only her word for it that the man had meant nothing to her.

There was his uncle, the sheriff. He and Bart had served under him and it looked like the old man had had no wish to go out against the Reeses even though they had killed his nephew. Maybe the sheriff was cautious, maybe frightened or maybe . . .

Willmore floundered in mental darkness.

Sure, he knew now what some of the Reeses looked like. But he didn't know all of them and he didn't know their hired men. He was like a man blindfolded, standing still while men got ready to take pot-shots at him. They knew him, they knew the country.

How then could he escape them?

The answer to that was plain. He would have to go clear out of the country, go where he wasn't known.

He realized that he had realized that answer for a long time. But he was strangely reluctant to go. He wondered if his feelings for the woman were stronger than he knew. Or was it that he knew the answer to the riddle that was himself lay around here and that he must stay until it was solved. However, there was no sense in solving a riddle if the answer was death.

There were a number of things that he would like to have asked his uncle, the sheriff. It seemed certain that Mrs. Craytham did not know him intimately. She had seen him and his brother in town, she had heard about them; she knew little first-hand.

He knocked out his pipe in the palm of his hand, stamped out the still burning tobacco and stood up. When he reached the old stoop it creaked under his weight. When he knocked on the door, it opened almost immediately. The woman stood outlined against the dim light within.

"Boys asleep?" he asked.

"Yes."

"I'd like to talk if it isn't too late."

"No," she said, "it's not too late. I'll turn the light down and come out."

A minute later she was sitting in the rocker on the stoop, her face pale in the moonlight.

"What did you want to talk about?"

"Me."

"I thought we'd talked that one out."

"Let's talk about my brother, then."

He sat himself on the steps.

"I hardly knew either of you."

"You must of known a few little things. Like, how did me an' Bart get on?" He wished he could have seen the expression on her face more clearly. He thought she frowned.

"You were brothers. Twins. Aren't they always close?"

"Maybe. Now, tell me: Do you reckon the Reeses still want me?"

"I can't know that for sure. But knowing them, I'd say 'yes'."

She went to say something more, but he held up a hand for silence. A faint shuffling sound reached his ears. The shuffling steps of a horse in dust. There was a rider approaching along the trail from the south and he was close.

He stood up quickly and said: "Somebody comin'."

Startled, she rose also.

He thought: *My gun's in the barn.*

"Quick," she said softly. "Get into the barn. You mustn't be seen here."

He limped quickly across to the barn

and stepped into the dark warmth of the interior from where he could see the moon-bathed yard and the entrance to the trail. He made it only just in time. Even as he reached out to where his gun-belt hung from a nail and his hand closed on the worn walnut butt, a horseman came slowly into view.

At first Willmore saw only a heavy bulk of a man on a big horse, then as the rider came slowly across the yard, he saw that it was the gross man he had seen riding at the head of the Reeses. As the man passed him, he took a pace forward and looked right toward the house. Mrs. Craytham was standing one hand rested against an upright at the head of the stoop steps.

The man halted six yards from her and tipped his hat brim with his fingers.

"Mrs. Craytham, ma'am."

"Mr. Reese."

"Your husband around?"

"No, he's not here."

The man cocked his vast head on one side. He hunched himself over the saddlehorn. His back was almost directly toward Willmore.

"Now, that's funny," the man said. "He rid off from our place yesterday and he said he was payin' his lovin' wife a visit."

Something in the gravel tone made Willmore's hackles rise.

The woman's hand went to her throat, fluttering white in the moonlight. She faced the man squarely, but the man watching from the barn knew that she was afraid.

"He didn't come here," she said.

The gross man slapped a big thigh and laughed hoarsely. "That's funnier," he said. "I'll be dogged if he ain't the sly one. Tellin' us he was comin' home and went off into town. Don't that beat all?"

Saddle-leather creaked as he heaved his bulk out of the saddle. He strutted to the stoop steps and looked up at her.

"It beats all," he said, "by golly, it does, him not coming home to a wife as pretty as you."

He started up the steps and she began

to move away from him, but one of his hands grasped her wrist. He said something in a low voice that Willmore could not catch.

Willmore stepped from the deep shadow of the barn and was bathed in moonlight. He called:

"Hold it right there."

Reese stopped suddenly as if he had walked into a fence. Surprise showed in every line of his body. Automatically he came around, placed himself between Willmore and the woman, which was a good thing from Willmore's point of view. His hand slapped down onto the butt of his gun, which was a foolish thing from his own point of view.

"Don't," Willmore said, tilting his own gun so that the muzzle was pointed at that gross gut.

He paced forward several steps till the man saw him clearly. Then Reese gaped and said in profound surprise: "Willmore."

Willmore halted.

"You thought I was dead, did you?"

Reese half-turned and stepped back a pace so that he no longer covered the woman. He glanced from one to the other.

"Bob Craytham," he said. "By God, woman, you lied to me. Bob was here. He had to be."

"He was," Willmore said. "He made the mistake of tryin' to kill me."

The fat man was frightened then. The flesh of his face shook. He had been shocked badly. He had a moment before thought that he had an attractive woman on her own, now he faced a man whom he and his family had tried to kill.

He fought to get a grip of himself and did pretty well at it.

"What happens now," he asked, "do you kill me?"

"You fork your horse and ride," Willmore said and watched the amazement blossom on the man's face. "Leave your gun." Willmore stepped up to the horse and heaved the carbine from its boot, flinging it into the dust.

"Hell," said the fat man grieved, "that ain't no way to treat a rifle."

"Unbuckle your belt and let it drop," Willmore told him.

The man obeyed and stood looking extraordinarily naked without the weapon. He looked bleakly at Willmore and said: "You shouldn't of done this to me, Willmore. You should of killed me."

"It isn't too late for that," Willmore told him. "Just tempt me. As it is I'm a good mind to beat your head in. Now get on your horse while the goin's good."

Reese stared at him for a moment, walked to his horse and slowly heaved himself into the saddle. He looked down at Willmore, but did not once glance at Mrs. Craytham.

"You don't stand a chance after this, Willmore," he said. "I promise you that. You're a dead man."

"Get movin'," Willmore told him.

Slowly he turned the horse, flicked it with his quirt and sent it at a trot down the trail. Willmore watched him disappear in the moonlight, put his gun in his belt, retrieved gun-belt and rifle from the dust and faced the woman.

"That *would* have to happen," she said. "Now they're on to you."

He smiled. "I would of had to ride pretty soon, any road," he said. He said it carelessly, but there was a deep worry in his mind. Again his lack of memory made a fool of him. He would be like an inexperienced child in this brush country. If he hid, the chances were that he would be ridden down by the Reeses in no time at all.

He went to the barn without another word. He hung the gun-belt in place of his own on the nail and strapped his own around his waist. Then he saddled the sorrel in there and put the bridle on. The animal was restive and excited by the chance of a run. He wondered what chance it would stand against the fine horseflesh that the Reeses owned.

The woman wasn't in the yard. The door of the house was slightly ajar and a faint light glimmered from within. He went to the door and knocked softly. The woman's voice bade him enter. He went in and saw the two boys asleep in their bunks. The woman looked up from the table and saw that he had his gun-belt on.

"I'll go now," Willmore said and that brought her to her feet.

"Now?" she said. "You can't go now. Wait till dawn at least."

"No," he told her. "It had better be now. We don't know how near the rest of the Reeses are and I don't want any more trouble for you."

She didn't say anything for a moment, as if she found it hard to realize that he meant what he said and was going.

"You'll want supplies," she said.

"No," he told her, "I'll make out." He didn't want to take from her meager store. But at once she was busy, putting food into a gunnysack. When it was full she bound its neck with a string and handed it to him.

One of the boys stirred and she beckoned for him to go outside. On the stoop he turned and she said: "The boys'll be disappointed."

"Say my goodbyes for me, will you?" he said. She nodded. "Now," he said, "I don't know what happens from here on out. Maybe one day I'll be able to come back. I would like to."

"Do you mean that?"

"I mean it. Now, thanks aren't enough for what you've done for me, ma'am. I shan't forget it. Maybe one day I'll be able to do something for you."

"Maybe if you come back we won't be here," she said. "We can't hold on much longer now."

That was plain. A lone woman in a brush-country ranch-house didn't stand a chance.

"One thing I never asked you," he said. "I was deputy-sheriff of this county. Was that all I did for a livin'?"

She raised her eyebrows. "Why no," she said. "You had your place of course. I never thought to mention it."

Suddenly he was excited and his heart was pounding.

"What is my place?"

"A house," she said. "Your father's old

place. Cattle, hogs, hens. Just like any place else."

"Where is it?"

"You can't go there. That's the first place they'll look for you."

"They will have looked there already. Where is it?"

She thought.

"Take the trail south out of here. You remember there was a fork in the trail three miles south of here. Coming from town you take the right-hand fork. That'll take you across Turkey Creek. About a mile north of the creek there's another fork. Take the left hand road and you'll hit your place about two miles on. You can't miss it."

He smiled. "I wouldn't bet on that," he said.

She said: *"Vaya con Dios."*

He took her right hand in his. He didn't say anything, because there were no more words to cover what she had done for him. He let it drop and walked to the sorrel and swung aboard. His right leg gave him a wince of pain, then he was settled in leather and it felt good to be on a horse. He lifted a hand in farewell. She did the same.

When he had turned the horse, he lifted it into a trot and didn't look back again.

7

MORGAN REESE sat on the stoop of the fine house and watched the horseman approach down the brush-road. He knew that it was his younger brother Bull. No mistaking that bulk even at half a mile. Morgan fanned himself with his broad-brimmed hat and not for the first time cursed the heat of Texas, cursed the ambition that had brought him and his family here. But this was where there was a fortune to be made. This was where the Yankees ruled and the southerners were beaten to their knees. Davis wouldn't be governor forever and by the time he stepped down and politics regained their norm, the Reeses would harvest what they could from the land of Texas.

So far they had done well. As Morgan had remarked so often in wry humor, they had arrived in Texas the year before with nothing but their carpet bags. Now they owned land enough for any man, ten thousand head of cattle and various business interests such as stores, saloons and a stage-line. Hamilton Reese ran a healthy freight-line. That was Morgan's cousin. Clancy Reese, another cousin, owned the bank.

His mind slipped to Tom Willmore.

There was a worry. The Reeses would never be sure of their conquests while there was a man like that running around loose. That was the worst of these damn idealists—they didn't know when they were beaten. Not even Bart's death had deterred the fool. Nothing would stop him except a bullet through the head. The Reeses had had bad luck the night Willmore had come alone to fight the whole clan. How gun-crazy could a man get? Coming here alone with a gun and trying to pay off the score of his brother's death. Willmore must be out of his head. If only he could be sure that Willmore was dead.

But Reese knew a twinge of fear when

he thought of the man. What could you do against a man who didn't have the sense to stop coming, against a man who was apparently unafraid of death itself?

Bull rode into the yard. His horse was bushed and he didn't look far off that state himself. He tumbled as clumsily as ever from the saddle, swore as he stumbled and came stamping up onto the stoop.

Morgan didn't need to be clairvoyant to know that something had happened. For one thing, his gun was missing.

"What the hell happened to you?" Morgan demanded. "You look like you saw a ghost."

Bull threw himself into a chair that complained under his weight.

"Maybe I did."

"What's that supposed to mean?"

"Tom Willmore."

Morgan sat up straight."

"Where?"

"Craytham's place."

Morgan looked amazed.

"What was he doing there?"

"Holding a gun on me," Bull snarled.

"What about Craytham?"

"Didn't see him."

"He must've been there. He rode home."

"Maybe he got there and maybe he didn't. For all I know Willmore killed him. But that's where Willmore's been hiding out. For sure. We hit him all right. He was limping."

They both turned as another horseman rode toward the house. This, they saw, was Clancy Reese, the cousin who owned the bank in town. It wasn't often that he came out here. He must have news. They didn't say a word till he dismounted and stepped up onto the gallery. He was a tall man with prominent bones, closely placed eyes and a way of assuming that he was always right. Even his few friends thought that he was mean. He had the air and clothes of a preacher. There was a musty smell about him. He rode a horse as though it were distasteful to him.

He nodded to them briefly and said their names. They were as curt in their own greetings. The Reeses were not men who wasted words.

Morgan asked: "You have news for us?"

Clancy sat on a chair, bolt upright, his hands on his knees and his eyes on the distant brush.

"I have. And you both look as if you have the same for me."

Bull said: "I'll say. I seen Tom Willmore."

Clancy jerked his thin head around on its long scraggy neck.

"It's him I came to tell you about. If you know he's alive, half my time's been wasted."

Morgan said: "Why only half?"

"Do you know about his memory?"

They gaped at him.

"Memory?" Morgan said. "What in hell're you talkin' about?"

He put his thumbs in the armholes of his vest and leaned back just the smallest bit.

"One of you creased him with a bullet. You know that?"

"Not for sure."

"Well," Clancy went on with a wry smile, "looks like the blow addled his brains a mite. He lost his memory."

He leaned right back and surveyed the effect his statement had on them. They looked at each other and Bull said slowly: "That accounts for several things, I guess."

"Such as?"

"Well, he looked kinda funny. Like he didn't know me. It had me puzzled. But now you tell us this, that explains it. Yeah, that's what he was like, a man that's lost his memory."

He leaned back against the gallery rail and slapped a huge thigh. "Son of a bitch!" he exclaimed. "This sure is rich. You see what this means?"

Morgan said: "If Clancy's right, it means he don't know any of us. He's as good as mutton."

They talked. The main purpose of their talk was to work out where Willmore was. What would a man who had lost his memory do? What could he do? They knew that he had been at the Widow Craytham's place, but they doubted that he would have stayed after coming face to face with Bull there. They knew from Clancy that he had been in town briefly, but they reckoned that he would think twice before going back there. He was out in the brush some place then, a brush that he could not know, not if his memory really had gone.

Morgan went to the edge of the gallery and bellowed.

"Waco!"

A few minutes later there came the shambling figure of the Waco Indian. One look at him in his dirty levis and shred of blanket was enough to tell the men on the gallery that he was more than half-drunk.

"Christ!" Morgan said in disgust, "where in hell does he find the stuff." The man came to the foot of the gallery steps and stood blinking up at him. His head turned and jerked; he dribbled. There wasn't much of the noble savage about Waco. But the Reeses knew what he was worth when it came to hunting a man.

"You're goin' to find a man for me, Waco," Morgan said. "And when you do I'm goin' to give you two bottles of whiskey. Two." He held two fingers up and the Indian grinned, moaning softly to himself and nodding in delighted anticipation.

"Me find," he said. "Goddam." That almost exhausted his English and certainly exhausted him. He squatted down and gasped.

"Bull," Morgan said.

"Yessir."

"The horses. Three, four men. One of them to be Regan. This is his kind of work."

Bull grinned.

"If it's Willmore, it's his kind of work all right."

He climbed down the gallery steps of the big house and went across the yard toward the corral, yelling men's names as he went.

8

WILLMORE came to a rise in the trail and halted. Here the road crossed at right angles the back of the highest ridge for a good way around. He had a good view of the country over the topmost branches of the tallest chaparral.

But he saw no house.

Maybe the woman had lied to him. Maybe he had lost his way yet, even with his addled brains her directions had been clear enough and he had obeyed them.

There was no house.

He had forgotten to ask her what manner of house it was. A big one, a small one; the house of a successful man or one inherited from a successful father. Or was it little more than a shack? Maybe it was too small to see from here. He sat the saddle, sweating gently in the overpowering heat, thinking about himself and wondering at his knowing so little of himself. Why, he did not even know his brand. Had it been Bart's brand, too?

He lifted the lines and urged the horse forward in a walk.

It took him thirty minutes to find out why he had not been able to see the house.

The charred rectangle showed him that it had been over a hundred feet long and in places fifteen feet deep. They had burned it thoroughly and hardly anything of even the big timbers were left. Here and there where the wall had been of massive adobe, perhaps the oldest part of the house built as a fort against Comanche and Apache, still stood. Here and there was a wisp of charred rawhide that had been used as hinges.

He dismounted and limped his way over to the remains of the corrals. The rail corral had been hacked down systematically and piled for firing, but they had not been able to do much about the huge old adobe one that had rested against the east wall of the house after the old way.

But the timber door had been torn down and probably dragged into the burning house. There was no sign of it.

The barn was a great charred ruin.

Whoever had done this had finished him with a vengeance. They were certainly thorough. These Reeses, if it were them, were certainly enemies worth having.

He looked around at the great sweep of pasture to the west and its surround of encroaching chaparral, hoping that the sight would evoke some memory, but it did not. He stood there motionless, straining at his memory, but all the effort brought was frustration and anger. These men had done everything to him, even taken away his past.

Somewhere a horse whinnied.

The sorrel colt lifted up its head and answered.

Willmore moved. He went to the sorrel, swung aboard and trotted it past the charred rectangle and rode it onto the great sweep of grass. There, almost in the center of it, facing him was a bay horse, head up, ears forward. Willmore reached forward and slipped his lass-rope free. He would see now if he was as good with a rope as he was with a gun.

When he was within thirty yards, the bay wheeled and broke away. Wilmore whooped to the young sorrel, raked home the spurs and went after it, building his noose as he went. He ran it clear across the pasture, through the broken rail on the other side and into the brush, ten minutes through the brush and then into a tangle of gullies where he let fly and caught the bay around the neck. It stopped without any trouble as soon as the rope touched its neck and stood waiting. The young sorrel didn't have either the sense or training to lean on the rope, so Willmore dismounted, took a purchase on it and walked along it, talking softly to the bay. The animal came to him and rubbed its nose against him. It was winded by the hard run. Willmore rubbed its nose and patted its sweating neck. The brand on its hip was the Flying W.

So that was the Willmore brand. The man felt better for knowing that. It did not ring a bell in his memory, but it felt good just knowing that. At last he felt as though he belonged to something and something belonged to him.

Both horses trumpeted as soon as the sound of the thud of horse's hoofs came to Willmore. Turning, he saw a rider coming at a canter across the pasture toward him. Willmore moved the bay around till it was between himself and the oncoming rider. Under cover of the animal, he drew his revolver and stood with it held against his right leg. He knew that by now word could have gotten around that his memory was gone. This could be a friend or a man who was taking advantage of his lack of memory.

As the rider came closer he showed himself to be a smallish man, raggedly-dressed mostly in leather and mounted on a roan horse. The face was seemingly shapeless and in deep shadow and this puzzled Willmore till the rider was close enough to reveal himself as a Negro.

When he halted his horse within ten feet of Willmore, the rider gazed at him in some wonderment.

"Boss," he said after a long pause, "you-all is alive. My Gawd, I done worrit myself to death wonderin' what in hell happened to you."

For a moment, Willmore knew neither what to do or say. Could it be that this man was one of the Flying W riders?

For the want of something else to say, Willmore said: "As you can see, I'm alive," and knew at once that he had spoken out of character. The Negro looked dismayed. The roan horse was restless and skittered this way and that, but not once did the rider's wide eyes leave Willmore's face. Willmore suspected that he knew this man well and that a warm greeting had been expected from him.

The Negro quietened the lively horse with a firm hand and stepped down from the saddle. He came toward Willmore who saw that he didn't carry a gun. They looked at each other across the back of the bay. The Negro halted and said: "I heard tell, Tom boy, that you sure 'nough lost your memory. That a fact?"

Willmore nodded and slapped the bay so that it stepped forward and left the two men standing face to face. He knew that this was a crucial moment and this man might be his first real ally.

"It's a fact," he said.

The Negro was, as far as he could tell, in his forties, whang-leather tough; his gun-barrel chaps and leather vest bore ancient scars from the brush. His face had been torn recently by a sharp thorn or branch. He was unwashed and smelled. The hand that he reached out instinctively to Willmore was gnarled and he had lost the top of his thumb which suggested that with a rope he was a dally man. But the hand never touched Willmore. The Negro hesitated and withdrew it. There was doubt and worry in his small black eyes.

"You don't forgot *me*," he said almost reproachfully.

I'd be made of stone, Willmore

thought, *if I doubted the sincerity of this man*.

"I forgot everything and everybody," he said, bringing the gun out from the concealment of his leg and slipping it away into its holster. He thought that the Negro's eyes would pop out of his head.

"Man!" he breathed. "You drawed a gun on old Mose."

"Mose," Willmore said. "Is that your name?"

"Mose Green."

Willmore glanced past Mose as the roan turned its hip into full view. The Flying W was marked plainly there.

"You a Flying W rider?" he asked gently.

"Flyin' W rider?" The eyes came wide and rolled. "Boy, I *is* the Flyin' W. All that's left of it nigh. I been Flyin' W since I was knee-high to a gopher. I rid for your daddy when he didn't have nothin' but ten dollar horse, fifty dollar saddle and a muley cow."

Willmore smiled, warming to the man. He held out his hand and gripped the

Negro's horny one. Mose was all smiles. He slapped Willmore on the shoulder.

"Boy," he said, "we don' hang around here. I don' aim to be caught by no Reeses way out in the open this way. I got camps a coupla-three miles. Leave us go there right now."

He got a hand on the bay's rope, untied it from Willmore's saddle and vaulted, spritely as a boy into his own saddle. Willmore went to the sorrel and mounted.

He led the way across the pasture toward what seemed at first to be an impenetrable wall of brush, but as they came close a narrow path was revealed. At a brisk trot Mose led the way down this, broke from the brush again and went through a jumble of wild and tangled gullies till Willmore had no idea which way they were headed. Then suddenly they came to water and a small prairie. Here a half-dozen horses, all nobbled, peacefully grazed. Mose dismounted saying: "I been roundin' up the stock."

9

THE fire was burning low. They had withdrawn their camp back several hundred yards for fear of the sound of the water drowning the sound of anybody approaching them. They had eaten and smoked together and had talked a long time. Mose Green had done most of it with Tom Willmore pushing in a question here and there. Mose was not a talker by habit, for he was a solitary man, more accustomed, if Willmore gathered the information right, to the company of horses, particularly wild ones. He was a mustanger by inclination and though he worked horses generally for the Flying W, his heart was with the wild ones.

Willmore's father had been a great one for horse-hunting, Green said. A great man, he told the son. They didn't make them like that often. He had come to Texas in the early days and held his place against the Comanches and the Mexicans. A man learned in the ways of men and cattle, a man of the wild places, a self-sufficient man whom apparently the Negro would have followed anywhere.

Slowly, Willmore gained the story from him.

First, he learned that the Willmore cattle had been considerable and probably still were. They had not been counted properly since the War Between the States. The war that Tom had come back from a battered and embittered man after lying wounded for two days after the battle of Black River Bridge. He learned of the Davis administration and how Texas's face had been ground into the dust of its loyalty to the Southern cause. The Reeses had come in from the north. Men said they were from Ohio, but Green reckoned that they had been in the West a long time. He, Tom, had told Mose that they had come from Comanche country, had ridden in from the Staked Plains after the War.

"I told you that?" Willmore said.

"You sure did."

"What else did I tell you?"

"Nothin' else about them, boy. You knowed more, but by Golly you wasn't tellin' ol' Mose. No, sir."

Willmore pounded his unwilling head with his clenched fists in his vain effort to remember. He must have known something vital about the Reeses and most likely Bart had too.

Mose continued his story. How the Reeses had had word from the north that cattle centers were being set up in Missouri and Kansas for the reception and shipment of cattle, how they had started to gather cows in their thousands and how they weren't too particular whose cows they were. That had started war between the Reeses and the Willmores. The Reeses had claimed unbranded cattle under the old unwritten maverick law that a man could claim all unbranded cattle as his own. All he had to do was slap a rope and a brand on them. They had ignored the also unwritten law that a man didn't touch mavericks on another man's land. The pickings had been rich. During the war the longhorns had bred prolifically and few of them had been branded. Mavericks ran in the brush in their countless thousands waiting for a brand. The Reeses had been busy. Mose reckoned they had more than twenty men riding for them and all of them cow-hunting. Already he reckoned they had over a couple of thousand head gathered, if he could believe the brasada talk.

"So," he ended, "what you aim to do, boy?"

Willmore stood up and put some more wood on the fire. It flared up and showed him the Negro's face grim in the flames. Mose was watching him and he knew that he was right to have faith in the Negro. Here was one simple man whom he could trust.

He squatted.

"You showed me what I have to do, Mose," he said quietly. "You started gathering horses carrying the Flying W. We gather all the cows with the same brand and anything that doesn't too."

The Negro grinned briefly and dazzlingly.

"You'm ma man, boy," he said.

"Mose," Willmore asked. "You reckon the Willmores have any money?"

The Negro looked surprised.

"Money? Wa-al . . . your pa was a careful man, sure enough. Most of hit went in the War, I reckon, but there must be a tidy piece left."

"In the bank?" Mose nodded. "Next thing we do is get it out. We hire riders. When the Reeses reach Kansas, likely they'll find a Willmore a-waitin' for them."

Mose looked troubled.

"Not so fast, *hombre*. You know who owns that there bank?"

"No."

"Clancy Reese."

"He can't stop me claimin' my own money."

"They jest ain't legal. They killed Bart illegal, they burned our place illegal. You reckon they won't stop you gettin' your money illegal. They don't have a thing to be scared of. Boy, you buck them and you'll have Davis's nigger cavalry down your neck."

Willmore looked at him and laughed.

"Mose, you know how to use that old Dragoon pistol of yours?"

"I should smile."

"Reckon that an' my Remington'll get our money?"

Mose laughed and slapped his thigh in delight.

"Man," he said, "now you sound like your daddy."

10

APPARENTLY Mose Green knew no more about town than Willmore did. He had no idea where Clancy Reese, the banker, lived and, as they intended only to go into town by night, it was his home to which they would have to go.

The first person to ask for help seemed to be Mary Willmore. For, after all who could be more trustworthy than his brother's wife. But neither of them knew where Bart's house was. So they decided on Charlie Willmore, the sheriff.

They rode in through Mex town around eleven on the following night. The place was as lively as day, stalls with flares burning near them lined the road and as they passed one courtyard Willmore heard the sound of a band of musicians and caught glimpses of the bright colors of the dancers' costumes. Mose rode close to

Willmore's side now and then touching his arm to indicate a man he knew—there that man yonder talking with the fat woman, that was Miguel Chavez. A Flying W rider. At a sign from the Negro, the man left his companion and hurried to the road. The two riders stopped. Willmore bent from the saddle.

"Chavez."

"Patron."

"We're gathering for a drive. Keep it under your hat. Can you be at the old place by noon tomorrow?"

"I'll be there. How about my brothers?"

Willmore looked at Mose. The Negro nodded.

Willmore said: "Bring them. But you and they must know that this enterprise will not be without danger."

The man grinned briefly and walked away.

Willmore straightened up and rode on, only then realizing that he had spoken without effort in Spanish.

Mose said with some satisfaction:

"Chavez and his brothers. Four good men. We have an outfit, boy."

"We need more."

"We'll git more. Let's first see if we have the money to pay 'em."

They clattered across the bridge and came into the Anglo's town. Here it was quieter, though still a couple of saloons on the left hand side of the street were being patronized. The sheriff's office was on the right. A light burned in the window. They turned toward it. As they dismounted, Willmore was aware of a man on the sidewalk leaning against the doorjamb. Mose tied his horse and came near to Willmore saying in a low voice: "That's Jake Stone. Bad medicine."

Willmore led the way through the open doorway. Charlie Willmore was sitting at his desk with his feet up. He still looked as if they were killing him. He looked startled at the sight of his nephew and gave Mose Green a look he must have reserved for mangy coyotes.

"Good evenin', uncle," Willmore said with a touch of irony in his voice.

The elder Willmore took his feet from the desk and the man who had been lounging outside came into the office. Tom Willmore turned and looked at him. He was a tall thin man, wirily strong with a long lugubrious face. He was not yet in his thirties, but his eyes belonged to an old and cynical man. On his shabby vest gleamed a lawman's badge. So this was the man who had stepped into either his or Bart's boots. Jake Stoner, the man who, according to Mose, was bad medicine.

Charlie Willmore put his hands flat on the desk and leaned forward. "What in Gawd's name're you doin' here, Tom?"

"I come to enquire about a man."

"You shouldn't be in town. It'll only cause trouble. You're my nephew, but even I can't protect you. You shot a man."

Jake Stoner leaned up against the wall. He seemed to have been born to lean. Willmore noted that he wore a pistol. Mose hitched his mammoth-sized

Dragoon around on his hip and sucked his teeth noisily.

"What about the man who shot Bart?"

The question seemed to hang in the still air of the office.

Charlie Willmore stood up and pointed a finger at his nephew.

"I hate to say this, Tom. I just hate to. But Bart got what he asked for. He went hellin'. He went out to shoot an innocent man down in cold blood. He forgot he was a lawman workin' under oath."

"Just why," Willmore asked calmly, "did Bart go a-huntin' Reeses?"

"He went clear out of his head is all. There ain't no other reasonable explanation. He went plumb loco. One minute he was a sober reasonable hombre, the next he was kill-crazy. Never seen ought like it in all my born days an' that's a fact. You, Jake?"

"No," said Jake, "can't say I have."

The voice was colder than water over stone.

"That sounds like a very reasonable explanation," Tom Willmore said. He saw the utter relief on his uncle's face. Then watched it fall away into frowning consternation. "I wonder if Mary'd give me the same explanation."

"Now you leave Mary alone," Charlie said quickly. "Don't you go a-plaguin' her on no 'count. She been through enough already, poor lamb."

"Not this trip, any road," Tom said, "but I reckon I'll get around to it. Right now I want to know where this Clancy Reese lives."

Astonishment showed on the elder man's face.

"Clancy Reese?"

Jake Stoner was moved to ask a question. He showed surprise too.

"What in hell you want for to see him for?"

"You keep your long nose out of this, Stoner," Willmore told him and watched the man stiffen in anger. Mose laid one black hand flat alongside the Dragoon and the man subsided, looking like a snake that had been trodden on.

"That's a fair question, son," Charlie

said in a slightly mollifying tone. "What could you want with Clancy?"

"Not that it's any of your business, uncle," Tom said, "but I'll tell you. I want to talk business with him. Any law against that?"

"Business? What business could a Willmore want with a Reese?"

"You're a Willmore ain't you, uncle?" Willmore hardly knew why he said that, but he knew he'd hit the button when he saw the look on Charlie's face. The older man went ashen under his tan.

"What's that supposed to mean?" he gasped out.

"Nothin' except what you make of it. Now do you tell me where Clancy lives?"

"You keep away from the Reeses is all I say."

"I can go out an' ask the first man out on the street."

The sheriff and his deputy looked at each other. Stoner nodded.

The sheriff said: "Carry on down Main and turn right into Whitley. Go along one block and it's the first house in the next.

Can't miss it. Neat white fence and gate. He lives good, does Clancy."

Tom looked both men over, nodded, said "Thanks" and walked out. Mose followed him.

They walked down the street without a word, stepping off the sidewalk and stumbling slightly over the ruts in the road. They turned right at the intersection and walked along one block. They found that Clancy Reese's house was a good one. Mose stayed on the street while Willmore opened the gate, walked up the neat yard path and knocked on the white door with the butt of his quirt.

It was opened after a pause of several minutes by a large woman. She looked sad, as any woman might married to Clancy Reese.

Willmore touched his hat to her.

"Good evenin', ma'am. I apologize for disturbin' you so late. Could I have a word with Mr. Reese?"

"A fine time, I must say, young man. Well, Mr. Reese is not here."

"Could you say where I might find him, ma'am?"

"You might find him partaking of a slight refreshment at the Southern Belle."

"Thank you kindly, ma'am."

He touched his hat and walked back to Mose. The woman stood watching him from the door.

"Luck's against us, Mose. He's at the saloon."

"Do we give hit a miss?" Mose asked.

"Do we hell."

They walked back to Main and found the Southern Belle still in noisy business. Outside, Willmore said: "Mose, go get the horses. Maybe we'll be leavin' the old home town in a hurry." Mose chuckled and went off.

Willmore looked through one of the two windows the building could boast.

This was not the usual brasada town saloon. There was a respectable bar running the length of the long room and there were two tables with chairs at them. Seated at one of these tables alone, a drink in front of him and a look of disapproval on his long face sat one of the men he had seen riding out of town. He took a gamble that this was Clancy Reese. There were some twenty other men in the place. Some of them were at the other table, but most were at the bar. The majority of them were cowmen, but there was a sprinkling of townsfolk.

Willmore went through the doorway and walked traight up to the man he had marked.

"Clancy Reese?"

The man was too startled to hide the fact. It seemed that the other men there were in a like condition. There was an immediate silence. Willmore had his back to the room, which he didn't like, and could see no more than a few of the men, but he knew that all eyes were on him.

Clancy went to get to his feet, but thought better of it. He settled back with fear in his eyes.

Willmore thought: *My bad luck if there are any Reeses behind me.*

"You keep away from me, Willmore," the man said softly in his fear.

Willmore half-turned and sat at the table so that he could see the room. Men started to look away, pretending that they hadn't stared. Clancy was to his right, so near that they almost touched.

"Let's understand each other right off," Willmore said. "I don't mean you any harm, but in case you're thinkin' of making a run for it or doin' anything else foolish, I have a man at the window with a gun ready to cut down on you."

"You must be out of your head to think you can get away with this."

"I know I can get away with it. I'm only here to talk business, man."

"Business?" The man was puzzled. "What business can you have with me?" His eyes darted around the room, desperately asking for help.

"Bank business."

"You have no business with my bank."

"What about my money in the bank?" It was a gamble. He had no idea if he had any money in the bank.

"There's nothin' of yours in my bank but Confederate paper."

110

The wide thin mouth shut like a trap in the cadaver's face.

"That's a lie and you know it." Again Willmore gambled.

"I could show you the books." Clancy didn't expect the offer to be taken.

Willmore surprised him. "Right, we'll do that." He stood up. Clancy craned his neck to look up at him.

"Go to the bank," he said. "This time of night. I could never permit that."

There was a short silence between them while Willmore debated on the wisdom of his next move.

"My gun," he said, "says you will."

Clancy swallowed and stood up shakily. "You're making a mistake. A terrible mistake. I am not without friends here."

"I have a gun," Willmore said. "My man at the window has a gun. That's enough for me. Let's go."

Clancy stared at him for a moment, looking as if his rage might get the better of his fear, but the fear won. He started across the room for the door.

A tall man with the unmistakable stamp

of a Reese on him, stepped away from the bar.

"Where you goin', Clance?"

Clancy stopped so suddenly that Willmore almost walked into him.

Clancy said: "Just over to the bank, George. Willmore and I have some business to transact."

"I'll come along," the man said.

"No," Willmore said. "You stay here."

"It's not necessary for you to come, George," Clancy said hurriedly.

George said: "I'll come just the same."

Willmore smiled.

"Let him come," he said, "if he's all that set on it." He turned to the crowd. "Anybody else want to join the party?" His question was met with blank stares.

Willmore turned, presented his back to them and walked out onto the sidewalk. Mose was at the tie-rail securing the horses. He looked up as Willmore appeared.

Willmore said: "Bring the horses, Mose, we're goin' to the bank."

The two Reeses stepped out of the

saloon. Willmore turned and they saw that he held his gun in his hand.

"I'll take your guns," he said conversationally, "just to be on the safe side."

George said: "You bastard."

"Say that again," Willmore told him in the same level tone, "and I'll knock your teeth down your throat." The man stayed silent. Willmore relieved him of his gun and searched Clancy to find that he didn't have one. He thrust George's weapon under his belt and put his own gun away. "Walk ahead of me."

They walked. Willmore followed three paces behind and Mose paralleled them on the street with the horses. They did not pass a soul on the way to the bank. Clancy opened the door with fumbling hands, found a match and lit a lamp on the counter.

"What now?" he asked. He looked calmer as if he were starting to suspect that Willmore did not intend him any violence.

"Get your books and prove that all I have is Confederate paper."

He saw that the place consisted only of one room. Clancy went behind the counter and heaved a great ledger onto its top. He fumbled through the pages and then prodded a page with a thin forefinger.

"There," he said, "does that prove it enough for you?"

Mose Green came in and stood just to one side of the door. George Reese looked at him with distaste.

Willmore said: "It proves I have Confederate paper. That was my father's. What about my money? I banked my pay as a deputy."

Clancy looked startled.

"No," he said quickly. "You never put a penny in here. I swear it."

Willmore felt depressed. So far as he could see, the man was telling the truth. He glanced at Mose. The Negro was looking savage. He took the giant Dragoon from its scabbard and came forward.

"You's too nice 'bout this, boy," he said. "Leave me work the barrel of this baby of his face a coupla times and he'll sing different."

"Keep out of this, Mose," Willmore said.

"Keep outa hit, hell," Mose said. "I'm in hit." His black hand shot out and grabbed Clancy by the front of his snow-white shirt. The Dragoon lifted. "Tell us the truth, you Yankee trash, or I start."

Clancy screamed.

"No."

George jumped forward. Willmore's gun swept from leather and, as the man's hands reached Mose, Willmore hit him across the side of his head with the barrel of his gun, knocking him across the room. He landed hard enough to shake the whole building. Clancy was beside himself with fear.

"No more," he cried. "My God, don't hit me. I lied to you. I'll give you your money. You must understand. After the shooting, you're an outlaw. You have no right. I'm not supposed to give you the money."

Mose let him go and he collapsed to

his knees. He put his hands together and wrung them.

"How much?" Willmore asked.

"I know exactly. Three hundred and twenty dollars."

It wasn't much, but it would buy supplies and maybe pay a few wages.

"Get it."

"Yes . . . yes." Clancy got his feet and hurried behind the counter searching for keys in his pockets. George groaned and rolled over. He lay on his face, moaning.

Clancy found the key he wanted and went over to a safe at the rear of the room. He was shaking badly.

George rolled over again and made a supreme effort to rise. Mose said to him: "Hombre, you put your head back on the floor or I'll bust it wide open." George laid his head down again and stayed still.

Clancy started to count notes out on top of the safe.

"I'll take it in gold," Willmore told him.

Reese looked as though a catastrophe had hit him.

116

"This is tantamount to robbery," he yelped. "You can't do this. Every man's hand in the country'll be turned against you."

"Get on with it."

The shaking hands took a poke of coin from the safe and counted out the right sum. Willmore picked it up and distributed it about his clothes. It was heavy and it clinked.

Willmore said: "Reese, you put a charge of robbery against me and I'll come back to see you. Don't fool around with me, I ain't in the mood."

The man stood there, glaring furiously at Willmore, mouthing the words silently that he dare not utter aloud. He looked a mess: his hair stood out in spikes and his string-tie was all over. He could hate and Willmore was too wise to underestimate the man's emotion. This man might be a coward, but he was as dangerous as the rest of the crew, that he'd bet on.

Willmore turned to the door, reached it and swung back again.

"Clancy," he said, "you put your nose

outside this door in the next couple of minutes and I'll shoot it off."

Clancy licked his dry lips and swallowed.

"I'm not a fool," he said.

Willmore went out onto the sidewalk with Mose close behind him. They went straight to their horses and swung astride. They went down the street at a brisk trot. As they passed the sheriff's office Charlie and his deputy stood on the sidewalk and watched them go without a word to them as they passed. They clattered across the timber bridge and went through Mex town into the brush.

11

THE following day, they left their camp and rode to what remained of the old house. Here waiting for them was Miguel Chavez and his four brothers. They were all small, tough men, clad in leather and mounted on good wiry ponies that looked as though they had spent their lives working the brush like their masters.

Miguel introduced his brothers. Willmore forgot their names as soon as he heard them. That was the way his brain acted these days. But he shook hands politely with each of them and told them in Spanish how happy he was that they were willing to come and work with him. He and Mose led them to the camp in the gullies, they all ate and then they talked.

Willmore put his propositions to them. There was a market for cows in Kansas, the north was beef-starved and Texas had more cows than it knew what to do with. It was late in the year to make a drive, but he was determined to do so. There was a chance to make money and he intended to take it. He put his cards on the table. Some or all of them might not want to come. There was little money for the project. He had enough to outfit them sparsely and he had enough so that each of them could leave a little with their families to tide them over till they got back. It would be tough work getting the cows out of the brush. Most of them had never been handled, the bulls had not been castrated and most did not wear a brand. But that was the least of it. The Reeses spelled trouble. The Chavez boys knew that the Reeses had burned the Willmores out and killed Bart Willmore, they had tried to kill Tom. They nodded —they were well aware of this and the fact did not frighten them. They were poor men and there had been no work for a long time. If Tom was willing to make the gamble so were they. What would they be working for? Money for their families now not to be charged against them. Thirty dollars a month and found and a bonus at the other end when the cattle was sold. Everything depended on the cattle being sold.

They looked at Miguel. His small black eyes looked hard at Willmore and Tom knew that he was being judged by the Mexican on the past that he could not remember. It gave him an uneasy feeling.

The man nodded. The unknown Willmore had not been found wanting.

"*Claro*," Miguel said. "I have always ridden for the Flying W. It is the best brand there is. We will come with you."

One of the brothers said: "Miguel to be segundo."

That was something that Willmore had not thought about. He looked at Mose and the Negro nodded his willingness. The possibility of trouble of the leadership was at once ruled out.

Willmore nodded and said "Yes."

Miguel said: "'*Sta bueno*. It is all arranged."

They talked over their plan of work,

what supplies they would need, whether they would need more men. One of the brothers knew where he could get a wagon cheap. How about horses? Mose said leave the horses to him. They smiled, knowing how the Negro was with them. Willmore started to feel good for the first time since he had had the crack on his head. He gave Miguel some money and told him to go into town and buy supplies.

Before Miguel rode off for town with two of his brothers, he and Willmore decided where they should make their first holding of cattle. There was, as the patron knew, Miguel said, a prairie three or four miles to the west of this spot. That was furthest away from the Reeses and the land was broken beyond it. There was water there at this time of the year still. It would be a good place. Mose agreed that it was so. It was decided that the four remaining men would wait for the other two before they began the cow-hunt. All hands would be needed for hunting and holding the cows.

Willmore, Green and the two Chavez rode west at an easy pace and camped that night on the edge of the chosen prairie. It took the briefest inspection to show Willmore that this indeed was a first-rate place for holding cattle. Mose estimated that there was enough grass here to hold several hundred cattle for over a week. He scouted around the following day looking for other holding grounds. They intended that their cattle should be numbered in thousands rather than hundreds and cows ate a lot of grass.

Very close to this open grassland, tight in the brush and handily concealed unless from the closest inspection, was a large holding corral. It was now in poor state of repair and the men at once got to work on it, for without it no cattle could be held. The wild ones from the mesquite would need to be penned in here at night to stop them from making a break for their old hiding haunts. It was hot, hard work, but fortunately the close brush was in aid to the strengthening of the pen and by nightfall the place would do at a pinch.

H9

In the dusk of the following day, by which time they had a full remuda of one hundred and sixty horses gathered with more to come, Miguel and his brother came in the wagon with the supplies. The wagon was not as good as it might have been but Miguel didn't seem to have any doubts that it would stay together to Kansas. He grinned and said: "Give me the hide of one cow, patron, and I will fix it like it was held together with iron."

They camped that night by the water and the following day spent choosing their horses, eight to a man, knowing that they would use up horseflesh in this heat. This was a time when men would have to prove tougher than horses.

The youngest of the Chavez, Chico by name, was voted wrangler. Then they started the hunt, all of them riding together into the south-eastern section of the land over near the edge of the country held by the Reeses. They would chouse cows out of the brush, sweeping westward, working their way first north and then south, continually moving away from the danger of the Reeses. The wagon they left back at their main camp with the remaining part of remuda.

The following day was a blur of hard riding, sweating, shouting and roping, in a heat that suffocated and wore men and horses down. In the deep thickets where the longhorns hid during the day, only coming out to graze on the prairies in the cool and safety of night, there was the heat of a giant oven. There was little air to breathe and the men were soaked with sweat and being brought to the edge of collapse by the time they were saved by the cool of evening. Now was the time when men could be found wanting. But none of the Flying W crew failed Willmore. Everyone pulled his weight.

By the end of the afternoon, though the men were worn down and the horses had been run into the ground, they had no more than twenty-five animals, bulls, cows, heifers, old steers, to show for their sweat. This method of working was gravely uneconomical and as they struggled to drive their catch to the pen and stop their frequent breaks for liberty, Miguel told Willmore that first they had to have some tame steers to help them and that there was no sense in their continuing the hunt in the heat of the day. At least not until they had skimmed the cream of the herds by night.

They lost three animals in the dusk and had the rest close-herded by full night. They never got half way to the pen and Willmore realized that they were doing this all wrong. There had to be a holding pen closer to their hunting grounds. They camped with three men continually on guard with the small herd, but even so they lost three more animals,. They were, one of the Chavez boys said, the wildest bunch he had ever seen.

The following day they choused the herd to the pen and after a battle of a couple of hours managed to get them inside. It was like getting peas into a pod. No sooner was one in than another was out. Again men and horses were worn down.

Willmore got the men together and

talked with them over a meal that Mose managed to get together for them. It was a good one, though scratch, and they all voted with much laughter that Mose should in future be their official cook. He protested furiously, but agreed until they could find another.

They decided that they should build another pen and talked over the best place for it. Mose Green knew that area best and he suggested a spot and the Chavez boys agreed.

After the meal four men rode into camp bringing with them a small pack of dogs. As they rode up, Mose whispered that these were the Carys and they were friends of the Willmores. The old white-head was Jim Cary, the others were his sons, Bill, Jed and Sam. They were all tall, rangy and tough. There was no doubt that they were brasada men. They bawled the dogs to hell and swung down from their ponies. Hands were shaken all around and the newcomers joined the circle for coffee.

Jim Cary sipped the black brew.

"Heard you was cow-huntin', Tom."

"Gettin' a trail herd together."

"Goin' to Kansas like the Reeses?"

"Yep."

"Got enough men?"

"No."

"How about me and the boys throwin' in with you-all?"

Willmore flicked his eyes to Mose and the Negro nodded almost imperceptably.

They talked. It was as simple as that. Men talked and accepted each other's words. The Carys would throw in with the Flying W and they would run a mixed herd north, each taking out the proportion they had put in. They shook on it. Then came some good news. The Carys had a dozen tame oxen they would help bring in some of the troublesome ones, the *ladinos*. Their dogs would help too. Old Jim couldn't think of going on a cow-hunt without his dogs.

The Carys were north of the Willmores and it was decided that the Flying W would merely extend their gather north and pen their westerly drive in the Carys' pens. That was a great saving and Willmore was relieved. He decided that his new pen could be more to the west. The Carys said that they would bring their own wagon. Old Jim reckoned he wasn't going to poison himself on old Mose's cooking. No, sir. If there was any cooking to be done around here he'd poison himself. His sons groaned, but he was adamant. He was too damned old to go traipsing around the country hunting fool cows. He and his sons departed, promising that they would be back the day after the next, bringing their wagon and supplies with them.

Mose grinned at their departing backs. "Boy, you sure has the luck."

Even Miguel was pleased. Things would go well now that the Carys were with them.

Things did go well. The Carys were good horsemen and good cattlemen. They were tough and they were desperate to make a success of the enterprise. And the old man could cook. The two younger sons,

Jed and Sam, were wild harum-scarum sky-larking young devils and even the hard riding they were called on to do did not rob them of enough energy to be fooling around at horseplay in camp at night. They were good ropers and Bill, the eldest, was a dab-hand at tailing the *ladinos* who played hell with the cowhunters. If a cow gave trouble and so many of them did and a busting on the ripe-end was not enough to cool its ardor, then either Bill or one of the Chavez boys would ride up on the running cow, grip it by the tail, kick a foot free from the stirrup-iron, throw it over that arm and rip the animal from its feet. One such performance usually left it gasping and chastened on the ground. Five minutes later it would stagger to its feet and be ready to be driven. If it was not, then the Cary lead-oxen were brought into use and the troublesome one was tied to it and the tame ox brought it home. One such fighting bull wore itself out fighting a tame ox and died fastened to its companion, killed by supreme effort in the fatal heat. It was butchered for meat and its skin stretched and dried in the sun for use as rawhide.

The pen in the center of the Willmore land was completed and after the Cary pen was filled, the hunters moved. The greater part of the brush-work was being done in the cool of night when there was enough light, but it now took three men at least to bring the herd out of the pen during the day for feeding and watering. As the gather grew so more men for the chore were called for. Willmore started to wish that he had even more men.

What they would have done without the Cary dogs, Willmore would never know. He had never used dogs with cattle before and at first had his doubts about their usefulness, but one day with the Cary boys and their animals was enough to make him change his mind. They were short-legged, stiff haired mongrels, but built like typical cattle-workers, just the right height to snap at cows' heels. They would flush a cow from cover quicker than any hard-riding cowhand could and were invaluable with herding. There were six of them and every one earned their keep.

By the tenth day, the center corral was filled and it was decided unanimously that it was uneconomical to keep the two pens going with men to look after the cows. So the northern bunch were brought down, mingled with the center herd and then the whole shebang was driven west to the large prairie, where the final and biggest gather would take place. By now they had gathered four hundred or more longhorns.

The drive was hard, hell on horses and men. The cattle did not yet consider themselves a herd and in spite of the dogs and tame oxen among them still were trying desperately to get back into the brush. The horses must have covered the distance a hundred times by the time they had them pushed into the main pen on the twelfth day.

It was decided then that men and horses had had enough. A day of rest would not come amiss. For one day they would do nothing except put the cows out to grass and water.

Willmore took the chance to go visiting.

He put on clean levis and clean shirt, borrowed a fancy bandanna from Bill Cary and declared that he was going visiting. Two of the Cary boys decided they would go to town and two of the Chavez boys thought they would go home and see their folks. The five of them rode south-east together in the direction of town.

Ten miles this side of town, Willmore left the others and turned east through the brush, headed for the Widow Craytham's place.

He found that he was oddly excited, more like a kid going to a dance than a grown man riding to call on a mother of two boys. He had a proposition to make to Mrs. Craytham and he hoped that she would accept. She must be finding things really hard alone on the ranch with no cash money coming in. There was the future to take care of too. He owed her a lot and this was one way of paying off the score.

When he rode into the yard, there was no one in sight. He halted in the center and called.

"Hello, the house."

She came to the door brushing the hair from her face with the back of her hand. She must have been working over the stove. Her sleeves were rolled up and her face was flushed.

She stopped almost in alarm at the sight of him. He threw a leg over the horn, slid to the ground and walked toward her. The limp hardly showed now. If you weren't looking for it, you wouldn't have known it was there.

He tilted his hat politely and said: "Howdy."

"Howdy," she said softly and looked down at him from the height of the stoop.

"You look kind of surprised," he said.

"Not surprised. Just taken aback, I reckon. I—"

"Didn't you think to see me again?"

She seemed lost.

"Several things. You look so well. I've never seen you looking fit. And there's the danger. I thought you were hidden out in the brush some place."

He laughed. He felt so good, he could have sung. He had known all along that he admired this woman, but seeing her even in her old work clothes and her hair all over, he knew that what he felt was more than admiration. It should have worried him a little maybe, but he felt so good he didn't give a damn.

"You been well?" he asked, suddenly shy.

"Yes."

"And the boys?"

"Fine. Just fine. They're around some place. They'll be crazy to see you. They've done nothing but talk about you since you went away." She suddenly remembered her manners. "Come up and sit in the shade. I have some lemonade. Would that be nice?"

"Fine."

She stepped back and he climbed the steps and sat down. She went into the house and came out with a jug of lemonade and two glasses. She poured and they drank. He finished his in one gulp and claimed more without a word being spoken. She sat down and he said: "I never did get around to askin' your first name."

She flushed a little and said: "Helen."

He thought he'd never heard a better name for a woman.

"Helen," he said, "a lot of things have happened since I saw you last. First, they burned my place to the ground. There's nothing left there."

Her hand went to her mouth and she said: "That's terrible."

"Not too terrible. I'm gathering a herd to take north. I have a crew, the best crew a man could have. The Chavezes and the Carys. We're all in it on a shares basis."

Her face lit up.

"I heard some talk about Kansas," she said. "Then it's true."

"It's true all right. The Reeses are gatherin' too."

"Is there still danger from them?"

"I reckon. But they'll be real busy right now."

"I'm . . . very happy for you."

"Thanks." They sat looking at each other, maybe looking a little foolish and he was thinking: *I wonder if she can feel anything for me, a busted nut without a memory.*

"Helen, I got a deal to offer you."

"A deal?"

"Yeah. What would you say if we made a gather of your cows and took 'em along with us?"

Her hand fluttered again.

"A gather for me? Why, I could never pay—"

"Nobody said anything about payin'. Nobody's payin'. Nobody has any money. I take your cows an' I bring the money back for you."

"I couldn't ask you to do that."

But he saw the hope in her eyes and it was like a tonic to him.

"You got to think of the boys. You must need the money."

"God knows I do."

"Then it's all fixed. When we've finished up on my land we'll head down this way." He laughed. "You'll have the whole place loused up with cowhands."

"I don't know what to say, how to thank you."

"I have to put it to the others. But I think they'll go along with me."

"I don't want to put you in a spot."

The boys came back then, whooping into the yard on their ponies at the sight of him and for five minutes he was all over boys. When they sobered down their mother told them about the proposed cow-hunt and they went crazy at the thought of there being one on their land. They begged Willmore to let them take part. He laughed and said he'd think about it. Maybe he could do with a couple of extra riders at that. Let them get in some practice with their ropes. They swore they would.

He rose to go.

She walked with him to his horse.

"I'll be back in two or three weeks," he said.

"Take care," she told him. "Because the Reeses haven't done anything yet, that doesn't mean to say they won't."

"I'll take care. You managing all right?"

"Sure, I'm doing fine."

They shook hands. He managed to pat one of her hands and get a smile from her, then he was astride and trotting his horse out of the yard. When he reached the brasada road he turned and the three of them waved to him. Then the house and the woman were out of sight.

His mind was entirely on the woman when the men in the brush made their try for him.

A rifle crashed and something thudded so hard into the saddle-horn that for a moment he thought that the horse had been hit.

12

SEVERAL things happened then, all of them too quickly to be separated one from the other.

The sorrel colt seemed to stagger sideways, to balk suddenly and then try to bolt. Another shot came and Willmore caught a glimpse of a wisp of rifle smoke against the dark shadow of the brush.

He did the only thing he could do. He ripped the young horse sideways and jammed in the spurs to make it jump for the cover of the brush. It obeyed almost too suddenly and blindly charged the chaparral, busting its way like a bomb through the almost inpenetrable wall. If it had not been for the cord, Willmore would have lost his hat at once. As a third shot came, he felt a branch rip cruelly across his face. He ducked his head down, crashed through a dense thicket, found himself in an open space and started to bring himself upright.

Something at once caught him in the head. He threw up an arm too late to save himself and felt the horse go away from under him. Instinctively he obeyed the teaching of his boyhood, kicked his feet free of the stirrup-irons and did his best to come down on his feet.

He hit the ground running.

One leg collapsed under him and he charged headlong into a tree.

For a brief second the world was sickeningly full of bright colors and stars. He clutched at the trunk of the tree and fell on his face.

He was at Black River Bridge. He could hear his sergeant screaming that the captain had been killed and that they should all get out of there. He lay on the ground and knew that he would never escape. Already he could hear the advance of the Blue Coats. They came cheering, their boots pounding on the hard ground. He lifted his head and saw the sun glinting on their bayonets. He was as good as dead.

When he looked the other way he saw his own comrades running, their butternut disappearing into the dimness of his own vision.

Then there was a man standing over him with a pistol in his hand. He saw the weapon distinctly—it was a Remington Navy Revolver. The man wore a coat of blue.

The man was named Regan Reese and this was the brasada of south-west Texas.

Another man came to join him and they stood looking down at Willmore and grinning. Their grins were like the wet-tongued snarls of wolves. This second man was immense and his name was Bull Reese.

In one startling and almost terrifying moment, Willmore knew that something extraordinary had happened to him. In that moment, he knew nothing of his memory. The only impression he had was that he had been hunting Reeses and now they were hunting him and had found him. He lay there for a full minute looking back at them, stricken by the unknown that had happened to him, vaguely aware that his memory was playing him tricks.

Regan said, the smile lighting his handsome face: "You should have left the ladies alone, Tom. I always told you they'd be the death of you. Not that I blame you. The widow's a damned handsome woman."

Bull laughed.

"Never thought you'd have to kill a man to get him off your woman, Rege," he said.

Willmore was lying on his right side. The gun was uncomfortable under him. He groaned and rolled a little and felt the butt come clear.

Bull put his gun away and said: "On your feet, Willmore." He took Willmore by the scruff of his neck and lugged him painfully to his feet. When he let him go, Willmore stood there, assessing himself, wondering if he were hurt and if movement would come easily to him. He saw the sorrel colt cropping the grass beyond the two men. Their own horses were near by.

"Before you kill him," Bull said, "I owe this son of a bitch somethin'."

"What makes you think I'm goin' to kill him?" Regan said easily, still smiling.

"You ain't goin' soft, are you?" Bull asked anxiously. "What in hell've we been huntin' him for?"

"First, Morg wants him. Second, he's goin' to hang legally and his uncle's goin' to do it. The situation is not without its amusing side."

"All right," Bull said, "but that don't mean I don't owe him somethin'."

"Be my guest," Regan said, turning his gun so that it was aimed at Willmore's belly. Willmore found that he was very calm.

Bull bunched his fist and raised it. It looked like the lethal weapon it was.

Suddenly he darted it at Willmore's face, but the tall man moved his head to one side with seeming slowness and the fist missed its target. Before Bull could recover himself, Willmore hit him hard in the stomach. The wind went out of him in a noisy gust. Then Willmore chopped down at him with the ball of his hand and knocked him flat into the dirt.

Bull started to rise almost at once. His face looked black from the ground and through the coating of dust his eyes glared wildly.

Regan said, cocking the gun, "Get back from him, Willmore."

Bull gasped out: "No, leave him be. I don't need no gun. I'll show you this bastard's lights before I'm done."

He advanced cautiously, crouched over looking like some monstrous bear. His caution availed him nothing. Willmore hit him in the face, getting a spurt of blood from the mashed nose. Bull bellowed and charged. Willmore sidestepped, tripped him as he went by and hit him alongside the left ear as he went by. He went down again. This time he took longer to get up.

"Don't be a damn fool," Regan said, "Give up, Bull, he'll kill you."

Bull rose slowly to his feet.

"Keep your nose outa this," he said and hitched at his pants, advancing on Willmore again.

When Willmore hit him this time, Bull flinched but he didn't fall back or go down. He continued to come forward, flatfooted and solid. Now he was at his most dangerous, as Willmore knew. The tall man drove his fist into the bloody face again and before he could withdraw, the great hand shot out and grasped him by the arm, spinning him around. He almost managed to wrench himself free, but the other arm clamped around his neck from behind like a vise. Willmore feinted by an attempt to throw Bull over his head and instead flung himself forward as though to fall face down on the ground. However, before he hit, he twisted and landed with Bull underneath.

Again the air went out of the fat man with a sigh of agony, the grasp around Willmore's neck was slightly relaxed and he broke free. They both managed to get to their knees from where Willmore slugged Bull in the belly, took a fist under the heart that nearly put him out, but managed a wild swing for the face which luckily connected. It wasn't strong enough to do much damage. Bull staggered to his feet, but, Willmore, slowed by the blow under the heart, stayed where he was trying to recover himself. Bull kicked him in the side and put him flat on the ground. He ran in and tried another kick, this time for the head. Willmore caught his foot, twisted it into agony and pitched the fat man over.

He went into Regan who tried in vain to get out of the way. Regan staggered, jumped clear of the fat man's flailing arms and legs and started to bring the gun to bear on its target again.

Willmore had his gun out. He fired and missed. Regan fired and had the same bad luck. Willmore cocked and fired again so fast that his shot sounded almost one with Regan's.

The handsome man was spun around, hurled from his feet and dropped to the ground. His gun fell a yard from him.

Willmore leapt to his feet and ran in and kicked it clear of the searching hand.

Bull got to his knees, his hand slapping down onto his gun butt. He froze when Willmore's gun came to bear on him. The rage slid from his face and was replaced by a sickening animal fear.

Willmore walked around behind him, lifted the gun from leather and tossed it into the brush.

"On your feet, both of you," he said.

Regan looked at him out of pain-filled eyes. He looked in a state of extreme shock. His face was ashen.

"I can't," he said. "I'm hurt bad."

"You're lucky," Willmore said without feeling. "I meant to kill you."

He came close to Regan and inspected him. The man had been shot in the body. Willmore ripped open the shirt and saw that the bullet, though it had made a mess, had done no more than glance along the right lower ribs.

"You'll live," he said in disgust. "Both of you get on your horses and ride. I don't have to tell you if I see either of you again, you're dead men."

Bull got to his feet. He was breathing hard. He was still scared, but not so much now he knew he would live. Some of his rage was seeping back.

"You damn fool," he said. "You don't stand a chance."

"Go on," Willmore said, "ride before I think better of letting you go."

Bull went and pulled Regan to his feet and half-carried him over to the waiting horses. He boosted him into the saddle and mounted himself. Willmore walked forward and heaved the two carbines from the saddle-boots. He tossed them after the pistols. This was the second time Bull had lost his weapons to Willmore.

They watched him with bitter eyes, Regan leaning on the horn of the saddle, his face drawn.

They took their horses away at a walk with Regan groaning as they went. Willmore put his gun away and turned to the sorrel. As he did so he caught sight of a movement in the sun-shadow. His hand snapped back to the butt of the gun as Helen Craytham walked from cover. In her hands she held an old single-shot scattergun. Her face was set and her eyes grim.

He smiled when he saw her.

"Were you there all the time in case I lost to Bull?" he asked.

She didn't think it amusing.

"I heard the shots," she said. "I rode one of the boys' ponies. I warned you about the Reeses. I suppose you were riding along dreaming."

"About you," he told her recklessly and she flushed suddenly and lost some of her grimness. "What Regan said . . ." he hesitated.

"About me?" She nodded. "I heard him."

"What exactly did he mean? Not that I have any right to ask."

"You don't have any right. But he meant that he comes to the house."

"Does that please you?"

"No, it doesn't."

He stepped to the sorrel and swung into the saddle. "Goodbye, Helen."

She lifted a hand and smiled. He rode on taking the memory of that smile with him.

13

WACO, the tracker, never fooled himself that he was a fighting man and when he heard Bull and Regan open fire on Willmore he lay low. He stayed low until all the trouble was over and calmly rejoined his masters as they rode away from their defeat at the hands of the lone man. He did not have to be told that they had been defeated and that their tempers were foul.

He rode out from cover and spotted the blood on Regan's coat straight off.

Bull and Regan halted.

Regan said: "Listen, you get under cover, fast. Tom Willmore comes this way, you follow him. I want to know where he's at by tonight. You got that?"

Waco nodded.

"Savvy," he said.

"Come on, Bull," Regan said and they both left him, getting off the trail as fast as they could so as not to run into Willmore if he came this way. They'd had their bellies full of Willmore for one day.

The Indian urged his horse back into cover of the brush, slipped from the saddle and tied up his horse's nose so that it would not give his presence away. He had no idea of which way the white man would go so he worked back to the spot from whence he had heard the sounds of the fight. He came on Helen Craytham and Willmore and sank silently to the ground to watch.

14

AS he rode away from her, he wondered why he had failed to mention to her that he thought his memory was being returned to him. As he rode, his mind probed her and her story, striving to remember all he could about her.

He knew with something like a dull shock that what he knew of her wasn't the most savory. She had been called for some years now the Widow Craytham for the simple reason that her husband was always away from home. It was also said that other men visited her during his absence and that he knew about this. He wondered if it were true that you couldn't have smoke without fire. But he remembered too the woman and the essence of her and he was willing to act and think upon his own judgement. She had saved his life. He owed her that much and that was not a light debt. She was beautiful and she was a good mother to her two sons. They were good boys and they would with half a chance grow into good men.

He knew also that he was a fool to have a woman on his mind when there was so much to do, but she stayed there just the same.

Then he remembered Mary Willmore and his uncle Charlie.

Now he knew that his memory was coming back. Helen Craytham's story was not the only unsavory one. His mind settled for the moment on the sweet-faced Mary and at once he knew that his memory was back with him with all its painful thoughts. Bart . . . poor blind Bart who for months had not been able to see what was going on right under his nose. But one day he knew. One day he caught Mary and young Jack Reese together and he had gone stark crazy—as any man would. The good-looking tough heir to the Reese fortunes had got away that time, but there could be no getting away from Bart once his rage was up. Bart had hunted him. For days. And had found him at the Reese house. Right there in the yard under the eyes of most of the menfolk of the family he had gunned Jack down. Jack had been good with a gun, but not good enough to face one of the Willmore boys.

He had done what he had come to do, but there was no getting away with it, of course. A tribe like the Reeses didn't see one of their members cut down under their noses, not even in a fair fight.

It was said that Morg and a cousin, Hamilton, had killed Bart.

There had been eight shots in him when Charlie Willmore went out to collect him. Eights shots, back and front. They must have gone berserk. Maybe Bull and Regan who had also been there had fired too. Willmore would never know. All he knew was that it was war between the two families from then on. And there was only one Willmore left.

Only one Willmore that would fight that is.

Charlie wouldn't fight. He was no coward, but he was a live-and-let-live man. A man who knew which side his bread was buttered. Willmore went cold when he thought of the risk that he had taken unawares when he had gone into town that day with Helen and gone straight to Charlie.

He lifted the sorrel to a run, heading back for the camp. He reckoned matters would come more into the open now and he wanted to warn the others.

He reached camp toward dusk when the boys were close-herding the animals back into their pen for the night. There was no chance for a talk. Dust and men were everywhere, the dogs were barking and chasing all over. The herd was still not a unit and though the leaders entered the corral, many tried to make a break back to grass and water. It was dusk and Willmore was sweat-caked and tired, before they finished and gathered around the fire. The other Chavez and Cary boys came in and then Willmore talked.

He recounted to them his whole story

and nobody's eyes were wider than Mose Green's when he realized that Willmore's memory had come back to him. The fact that Helen Craytham had taken Willmore in and saved his life stood her in good stead with these simple cowmen and without any disagreeing vote they said that they would make her gather for her and take her cows north. The more the merrier.

"What I'm gettin' at, men," Willmore ended with, "is that because of me we're all in the same kind of danger. Not only are the Reeses mavericking our cows, as Mose will tell you, but they are personally out to get me and if you're with me that must go for you too."

Old Man Cary spoke.

"Son, what you say's true enough. Far as it goes. But you ain't the only one 'at's been mavericked. There's plenty of Cary cows in the Reese herd. Hell, the ways them boys of been goin' to it, I reckon they aim to drive over five thousand north. Five thousand. Look at it which way you like, that's a tidy piece. No, it's best this way. We all have a stake in this. We stick together. Any road, no Cary ever backed down from a fight yet an' the Willmores stood by us when we first came into the country. I knowed your pa when he was younger'n you are now. We was friends. We stick."

The sons all murmured their agreement.

They all went to their blankets with a new feeling of unity.

Waco turned back to his horse from the brush at the edge of the prairie and headed for home fast.

15

WACO brought his news to the Reeses when they were seated at dinner in the big house. They always did this in style, Morgan at the head with his wife, a hard-faced Ohio woman at the other end of the long table. There were eight Reeses here in all and these referred to themselves as the Fighting Reeses to distinguish themselves from such men as Clancy Reese who were known as the Thinking Reeses.

Regan was there at Morgan's right hand, looking pale, but with his ribs strapped up with plaster and feeling not too bad though still a little weak from loss of blood. They were all dressed in dark suits and wore white linen as was their habit when they sat at Morgan's table. It was like a royal command. Even Bull sat sweating and choking with a tight collar. There were a couple of wives there, not saying anything. The Reese household was a masculine one and women didn't carry much weight in it. In town it was even hinted that Morgan chose their women for the younger members.

Nobody mentioned it during the meal, but they all knew, including the Mexican servants, that this was a council of war. As soon as the eating was done and the women had left, the drinking started and with it the really serious talk.

Morgan, naturally, began it.

They all drew close to him at his end of the table and he leaned back and sipped his whiskey. He looked flushed and grim and they all knew that they had not been called here for nothing.

Morgan said: "You all know what happened to Regan and Bull today. Well, Waco has come back with some news for us. Listen good and then ask questions if you want." He looked around him at them all and bent them to his will afresh as was his habit by the look of his eyes. "He found for sure that Willmore has a camp over by Luck Creek. He also has close on to five hundred head penned there. Many of 'em unbranded." He smiled as they looked at each other significantly. "I see the point is not lost on you. He also tells me that the Chavez from Mex Town and the Carys are in with him. That gives him a considerable force. They are all good men and handy with a gun. It therefore behoves us to use our heads. We don't just ride in there and shoot the butts off them. We use strategy.

"We all know the pattern of cow-hunts in this country. They have the cattle penned and during the day they loose them for water and grass. They leave some riders in charge of them while the rest go gathering more wild stuff. That's our chance. We hit the camp when it is weakest."

Regan asked: "When?"

"Tomorrow."

"Do we make a fight of it?"

Morgan smiled coldly. "You know me better than that. Who fights when he can run away? No, we scatter the herd, smash

162

the wagon—stuff like that—and get the hell out of there."

Bull said: "Where's the profit in this for us. All them unbranded cows."

Morgan turned on him angrily.

"There's the distance to be considered here. Use your sense. How can you lift their mavericks and then drive them all this way? Willmore'd be onto you before you got five miles."

Bull glared back at him.

"We have guns, don't we? I don't see the sense in all this. Sure I owe that bastard Willmore something, more maybe than anybody but I don't see no Goddam sense in riskin' my hide without no profit in it."

"You're crazy," Morgan told him.

"So I'm crazy. I'm crazy because I don't see no sense of doing something without no purpose."

Morgan looked at him coldly.

"A Reese was killed."

Bull leaned forward over the table.

"Ask the others what they think. Hell, we have to make up a trail herd. Where do we get the cows if we don't go maver-icking. Every damn cow we have is gold in the pocket. I ain't trailin' north with anythin' under three thousand. An' where do we get that kind of a herd in the time. It's gettin' late for trailin' now. I say put off this raid for another week. Let 'em gather all the cows in the world, then lift 'em. Get 'em before they carry a Willmore brand."

Morgan looked at him in silence, prom-ising himself that he would have to do something about Bull. He shot off his mouth altogether too much.

He turned to the other members of the family and asked: "Anybody else feel like Bull about this?"

Young Loge Reese, Morgan's nephew and Clancy's son said: "You bet. Let's go get their damn cows."

Regan said: "Shut your mouth till you're told to speak."

They all stared at Loge and he subsided, boiling. He did a man's work, why shouldn't he speak with a man's voice?

"I reckon Bull has something there, Morg. We don't have all the time in the world. We need cows."

A gray-haired man with a heavy white mustache spoke from the far end of the table. He bit off his words as if he had distaste for them. This was Henry.

"We got to hit 'em quick before they start brandin'."

Bull smiled, relieved that he had Henry with him. Henry was the man handy with guns. The cold fish of the family. A second cousin of Morgan's. If it wasn't for Morgan, Henry would be their accepted leader.

Morgan sat digesting his small defeat. They had gone against his judgement, but he would still lead them.

"Who do we use?" he said.

Bull said: "Me an' Henry. Young Loge. We'll hit 'em and put out a rear-guard to cover the cows. Barlow can have half-dozen hands to manage the cows."

Barlow was their straw-boss, the man who acted under the Reeses in control of the ordinary hands.

Morgan nodded.

"We'll do better than that. We'll all go along. We might as well do the job thoroughly. Regan, you fit to ride?"

"Fit or not, I'm goin'," Regan said. "I'm going to plant a bullet right through Willmore's eyes."

Bull laughed.

"He's mine," he said.

Regan merely gave him a venomous look.

Morgan leaned his elbows on the white cloth.

"Give me two or three days. I want Willmore out of the way. I'm not forgetting that the man's without his memory. Charlie Willmore tells me that when he spoke with Mary he was friendly to her. That shows he has no memory." They all laughed. "Give me a few days and we'll have Willmore in a cell waiting to have his neck stretched. I like to do things legal." That got another laugh. They agreed that he should have his few days. He told young Loge to have his horse saddled at dawn the following morning.

He was riding into town to see a lady. They knew the lady was Mary Willmore and they all reckoned they could see which way his mind was going.

The following morning, Morgan Reese rode into town on his fine bay horse. He took a couple of riders with him because it was his habit never to ride through the Texas countryside unaccompanied. He was wise, for the Reeses were not without enemies. Already their mavericking habits had been called to account by smaller men than themselves and the disagreement had been settled with violence.

Morgan rode into town a couple of hours after dawn and dismounted outside Mary Willmore's house. He spent an hour with her. She was young and attractive and Morgan was a little jealous of the attention she had been giving Regan since her lover had been killed by Bart Willmore.

She walked to the gate with him and said: "Don't you fret, Morgan, I'll do just what you ask."

Morgan smiled as charmingly as he knew how.

"You're a fine girl and a sensible girl, Mary." He thought that it was a great shame there was such a difference in their age. He compared her with his wife and found his own wanting. "I shan't forget you did this for me."

She smiled and said: "We don't see enough of you in town, Morgan."

He positively smirked as he mounted his horse and bade the two riders to follow him. He went next to call on the sheriff to give him his orders. When he had finished with the sheriff, he rode home. Here he set Waco to watch the round-up camp. He had to know when Tom Willmore rode into town or the whole plan would fall through.

He was pleased with himself as he went into the house and found Regan lounging there.

"Why aren't you out with the men?" Morgan demanded.

"I'm hurt or had you forgotten?"

"A graze."

Regan ignored the remark. "Did you see the girl?"

"Yes. We're all set. She'll get word to Willmore. And while we're on the subject of Mary, you'd best make up your mind who you're chasing. Her or the Craytham woman."

Regan stood up from his chair.

"You may run the business side of the family, Morg," he said dangerously. "But keep your nose out of my private affairs."

Morgan chuckled unpleasantly and walked away to his office, leaving Regan wondering what he was up to.

16

MARY WILLMORE stood at the window of the bedroom she had shared with Bart and looked down into the street. She was deep in thought, her lovely young face shadowed. She was depressed, for her life seemed to have ended before it had begun. She and Bart had made a mistake and Bart had never had the sense to admit it. When she thought of him, she was enveloped by an overwhelming sadness. He had not been a bad man, only tough and a little wild, without the underlying gentleness of his brother Tom. But he had loved her and been faithful to her. If she had not met John Reese she might have remained faithful herself.

He had been different from his kinfolk. He had seemed to be cast from a finer mold. He had been considerate of her feelings, thoughtful in the small ways that a woman liked. She had never known a man like him before. The tragedy was that she had met Bart too soon. Now both he and John were dead with the result that the whole town, including Charlie Willmore, the sheriff, thought that she was a Reese by adoption.

She lived from day to day now in a perpetual state of uncertainty with no idea what she should do next. She was young and inexperienced and had no older person to turn to. She was living on the small amount of money that Bart had left in the bank. It would not last so much longer. She had no idea what she would do when it was gone.

She was thinking now of what she felt about her brother-in-law, Tom.

It was a curious position. The man had lost his memory and might still be ignorant of what had happened. Morgan Reese might be right; Tom could still think that she was loyal to the Willmores. The Reeses certainly thought that she was loyal to them. John had gotten himself shot for her hadn't he?

She wondered herself where her loyalty lay and did not know what to answer except that she knew that she didn't have it in her to do Tom any harm. Morgan had merely told her that the law wanted Tom, but she could see further than that remark. The Reeses would see that he hanged. But she dare not warn Tom so that he did not come into town as Morgan wanted. She was under no illusion of just how dangerous the Reeses could be if she went against them. The fact that she was a woman would not protect her. She knew the Reeses.

Therefore, she had to fulfil her part of the bargain and Tom had to be brought into town. But how was she to do that without getting him caught?

She caught sight of Charlie Willmore tramping at an angle across the street toward her house. She wondered what motivated the man. Was he a coward or had he thrown in with the Reeses because he had never liked either Bart or Tom? Had the original quarrel been between Charlie and his brother, the boys' father?

She watched him enter the yard and was at the front door before he could knock.

"Mornin', honey. My, you're a sight for old eyes this mornin'." He gave her a fond smile.

She returned it and said: "Hello, Uncle Charlie, you're early this morning. I was just going to have coffee."

He laughed.

"What do you think I came for?"

As she turned away from the door, he threw an arm around her shoulders and gave her an affectionate hug. He smelled of tobacco and something else that proved he had taken a drink of liquor this early in the morning.

They went into the kitchen and they talked of this and that while she made the coffee. When she had poured it and he had taken his first sip, he made appreciative noises and said: "Nobody ever made coffee like you, my dear."

"Don't try and kid me you only came here to drink my coffee," she said playfully. He gave her a nervous glance. For a moment he looked a very worried old man and for that moment she knew pity for him.

"Wish I did," he told her. "By God, I wish I did, girl." He stirred his coffee, lost in thought. Suddenly he jerked up his head and said: "You're goin' to think badly of me, Mary, and I don't like the idea of that."

He looked so sincerely worried that for a moment also she believed in him.

"Do you have something on your mind, Charlie?" she asked.

"Didn't sleep a wink last night, thinkin' about it. Blood's thicker than water, say what you like, but a man has his duty. There're times when I wish to heaven I didn't have this star on my vest. Yessir, there's times when I reckon I'd of done better to stick to the cattle trade. That's where I belong."

"You worried about Tom?"

"You hit it right on the head first time. It's murder, child, an' there's no gettin' away from it."

She decided to come out in the open,

but even as she spoke she wasn't sure that she was being wise.

"Morgan Reese came to see me."

"I know."

"You know what he wanted?"

"Yes. An' you gotta do it, girl. You an' me'll hate ourselves for doin' it, but it has to be done. Maybe the Yankees're sittin' on Texas, but that don't mean that Texas men can act without due regard to the law. The law's above everybody."

He still sounded sincere. He looked her straight in the eye. She was impressed in spite of herself. But just the same she knew that she could not give Tom into this man's hands so that the Reeses could dispose of him.

"I have to do it," she said.

"Yes, you have to," he agreed, deep regret in his voice. "You know where Tom's at?"

"Yes. He's gathering on Lucky Creek."

The sheriff looked surprised and Mary wished she had kept her mouth shut. Charlie hadn't known that Tom was holding a round-up. The sheriff said softly: "The damned fool."

He finished his coffee, wiped his mouth on the back of his hand and rose.

"Young Jedson's your best bet for carrying your message, my dear. Tom thinks the world of little Jimmy." The sheriff smiled benignly. "Now, don't you go blamin' yourself. A person has to do things that go against the grain in a line of duty in this vale of tears." He came over to her and patted her on the arm. He looked into her eyes, his own filled with sincerity and pushed up her chin with a forefinger. "Chin up now and keep smilin'."

She walked with him to the front door, feeling nauseated. For the first time since first knowing him, she actively disliked Charlie Willmore. Nobody could ever have guessed that he was kin to two men like Bart and Tom. She watched him walk down the street toward his office.

Later in the morning, she wrote her note at her bureau and went out to find Jimmy Jedson. He jumped at a chance to ride her little mare and, having obtained his mother's permission, before noon was raising the dust for Lucky Creek.

Young Jedson was a mite let down when he found nobody at the camp on Lucky Creek but old man Cary. The old fellow's tongue was sharp and though he was liked by his contemporaries, the young walked carefully with old man Cary.

As the boy slipped from the saddle, Cary roared: "Goddam you to hell. Dust in my stew. Get that God-damned hoss away from my fire afore I lay my hand across you."

Jimmy backed up, freckles rampant, incensed but wary, knowing that he was in the wrong.

"I got a message for Tom Willmore."

"Who?"

"Tom Willmore. You deaf, Mr. Cary?"

"No, I ain't deaf. I just didn't hear no mister when you mentioned Mister Willmore's name."

"I got a message for him any road."

"Wrote?"

"Yeah."

"Give it me."

Jimmy backed up a little more. "I have to give to him and him only."

"Then you wait till nightfall."

"Where's he at?"

"How in hell should I know? Chasin' cows over hell's own half-acre. You wouldn't never find him in that brush in a month of Sunday's. Take the saddle off'n that fool pony and set. Here comes Chico now for his grub. You might as well eat with him now you're here."

Jimmy off-saddled and sat. There followed for him the most enthralling time of his life, sitting in a cow-camp talking cows and horses with old Mr. Cary and the cowhands as they came in from the herd. He ate till he nearly bust and was a very tired and sleepy boy when Tom Willmore finally rode into camp long after dusk. Willmore greeted him warmly, tussled his hair to his great annoyance and read the note. He frowned and walked away beyond the firelight. He seemed gone a long time to the boy who had nearly dozed off by the time he returned. He looked up at the tall man and saw that he looked grim.

In a kindly voice, Willmore said: "Throw your hull on the mare, kid. We best get you home to your ma or she'll skin me."

Old man Cary said: "Goin' into town, Tom?"

"Yeah. I'll be back before dawn."

The old man looked worried.

"How about some of the boys ridin' along with you-all?"

"No. We won't make somethin' out of this."

Willmore saddled the sorrel which was fresh and he and the boy headed for town.

It was an uneventful ride with the boy chattering twenty to the dozen. Tired from his hard day's riding Willmore half dozed in the saddle, knowing that nobody would make a move against him till he reached town, if indeed this note was a trap. A mile short of town, Willmore drew rein and drew the letter from his pocket. On the back of it Willmore wrote an answer with a stub of pencil.

"Jimmy," he said, "you only saw me at the camp. I never rode back with you. You give that to Mrs. Willmore, then hightail home. Tell your mother I'm sorry to keep you so late."

Jimmy looked askance, then said: "Sure will, Mr. Willmore." He rode off toward town.

Willmore watched him out of sight around a turning in the road, then turned his horse down a narrow side trail, little more than a narrow track. It curved right and left, but led him after a mile or two to the edge of the creek. He ranged along this for about a hundred yards, then forded it. The water was no more than above his horse's hocks. On the other side, he took the sorrel deep into the brush, dismounted, loosened the girths and went forward on foot.

He came to Mary Willmore's house from the rear.

It gave him a queer feeling, creeping up on Bart's home like a thief. He wondered what sort of a reception he would receive. Once he thought that maybe he was a fool to trust Mary at all, but he knew that he did not. He trusted nobody much any more. But Mary was Bart's widow and he had to give her the benefit of the doubt. Maybe she was in trouble as her note said.

Between the brush and the house was the trash that found its way to the outskirts of such small towns. Then there was her rear yard and the odds and ends that a man gathers over the years. He stumbled on a wagon wheel lying in the moon-shadow and then was at the rear door.

He tried it and it was open. That was not strange. A woman didn't usually have need to lock a door in this country. He went into the kitchen and his spurs made a little noise. He opened the door leading to the hall and saw a light coming from a front room.

As quietly as he could he went down the passageway at the side of the stairs and peeked through the crack in the door.

As far as he could see Mary was in the room alone, sewing.

He stepped into the doorway and said: "Mary."

She jumped in alarm and as she stared at him, the color left her face.

"My God," she said, "you startled me."

"Don't get up for a moment," he told her. "Wait a moment, then get up and walk naturally out of the room."

She waited a moment, not taking her eyes from him, then put her sewing down beside her and rose. As she came toward him, he saw that she was trembling violently.

As she joined him in the hall, he touched her forearm and found that she was ice-cold.

"Heavens, girl," he said, "there's no call to be scared of me. You know that."

She clutched at his arm.

"I'm not scared of you, you great fool." He put his arms around her and she drove herself against his chest. "You don't know how good it is to have you here.

Listen, Tom," she leaned back from him and tried to see his face in the uncertain light from the room, "there's a lot to say and we don't have much time. I'm going to talk fast and don't you interrupt me."

"Listen, Mary, are you really in trouble?"

"Not me, you. You lost your memory and I have to fill it in for you. You don't know what danger you're in. I had to send for you, but it's a trap and you'll think the worst of me."

He smiled.

"You don't have to fill in my memory for me."

"Will you listen? You're in danger. Your uncle—"

"You don't have to fill me in on Charlie or anybody else. I remember everythin'."

Her face was utter astonishment.

"You mean you came here for nothing?"

"I thought you were in trouble."

"And even with your memory you still came?"

"I reckon."

"Then you really are a fool."

"I can go like I came."

"The sheriff and his deputy will never let you. Tom, you can't afford a fight with the law. You're in trouble enough as it is over me."

"It wasn't over you."

"If Bart hadn't—"

"It's too late to go over all that."

"Then go now while you still can. Please, Tom."

He released her.

"All right. I'm makin' a gather, girl, did you know?"

"I know."

"You'll get Bart's share."

She was weeping now.

"I'm no good an' you don't owe me a thing."

"You fell in love with a Reese. That wasn't so much bad as poor judgement, I guess."

"Go," she said, pushing him away, "go for the love of God. I don't want another death on my hands."

He touched her face with his rope-gnarled hand and said: "Look out for yourself, Mary," and walked back through the house.

He paused at the back door, drew his Remington and checked the loads with his fingertips. That done, he opened the door quietly and stepped out into the full flood of moonlight.

Very close a man said: "Drop your gun, Willmore."

He drove a shot at the sound, jumped to one side and heard the other man's shot slam into the back of the house.

His instinct was to run for the brush and so get to his horse, but as soon as he started in that direction he heard another shot and muzzle-flame pierced the darkness ahead of him. He ducked back toward the corner of the house, not wasting another shot and only wanting to get out of there. His body was a dark target against the white paint of the building.

Another shot came and a window collapsed inward with a crash and a tinkle of breaking glass.

He reached the corner of the house and a fourth shot chipped the corner of the place. Even behind the safety of the corner he did not pause to give his attackers another shot, but ran on, favoring his still weak leg a little now that he was tired. It was a curious feeling running through the dark and not know where or how many his enemies were. At any moment he expected more to show up from another direction. If this was Charlie Willmore's doing, he could not believe that the sheriff had gathered all his forces at the back of the house.

But it seemed at first that he was wrong. He ran across Mary's yard, vaulted her picket fence and started across the next yard without any further sign of danger. It seemed that the guns behind him had given up and become silent.

He stopped in the shadow of a tree and thought quickly. He could try for the brush and his horse now, but that was what they might be reckoning on after his first attempt to escape that way. No, he would cross the street and get out of town along the bank of the creek.

He crossed the yard he was in and climbed the low picket fence. Main lay broad and long before him.

He put his gun away and started to walk across with as much casualness as he could summon. The flesh at the nape of his neck and down his spine crept as he waited for a shot to come from behind. He reached the centre of the street, in full view in the bright moonlight headed for the comparative shelter of the moonshadow of the overhang of Newnham's Store. Twenty yards further on up the street toward the creek was an alleyway. This would take him out through the backlots and to the water.

He was two-thirds of the way across the broad way when he saw the glisten of metal in the deep shadow and a voice said: "That's far enough, Willmore."

At once he recognized Clancy Reese's voice and he knew that this was where the banker got his own back. He knew also that Clancy wouldn't be in this on his own. An even fight would not be the man's style at all.

Willmore came to a halt.

"What is this, Clancy?" he asked in a neutral tone.

"This is a citizen's arrest, if you must know," came the reply. "The sheriff has a warrant for your arrest."

"I don't have to ask the charge."

"You don't and it's murder."

A man appeared twenty feet to the right of Clancy's voice. In his hands he held a twelve-bore shot gun. It was levelled at Willmore who knew that he would be blasted into blood-red shreds if he made a wrong move. The old calm of the gunman deserted him in that defeated moment and he knew only the black bitterness of despair.

To his left another man appeared. He carried a short carbine like a Spencer. Willmore had been suckered as easily as a greenhorn. He had got all he deserved.

Clancy appeared now. He wasn't smiling but he looked as pleased as a dog with two tails.

"Very neat," he said, "though I say it myself."

Willmore became aware that men were walking across Main from behind him. The men in front of him closed in and his gun was lifted from his belt. With the going of its comforting weight, he knew that he was finished.

From behind he heard Charlie Willmore's voice: "I'll take over now, Clance. Thanks for your help."

Willmore turned his head. Jake Stoner, the deputy, was there too. Both men had guns in their hands. Charlie was very close and Willmore could smell the whiskey on his breath.

Stoner said: "Let's go, Willmore. Just try somethin'. I'd like that."

One of the men with Clancy said: "Here's his gun, Charlie," and the sheriff took the Remington and pushed it down under his belt. He shoved Willmore and they walked along the street together with Stoner warily off to one side. Willmore knew that there wouldn't be a chance to get out of this with Stoner around. The man was a professional.

They reached the sheriff's office and Willmore was pushed inside. Stoner opened up a door to one side and Willmore saw the two cells beyond. Stoner searched him thoroughly then and he was glad that he had left his money with the wagon back at camp. The deputy took his clasp knife and his ammunition. In the right hand pocket of his vest he found the spare, loaded chamber that he always carried for the Remington. The deputy laughed shortly when he found this. Willmore watched him put the effects into the drawer of the sheriff's desk.

Charlie said: "You don't know how I hate to do this to you, Tom." There was real regret in his voice and eyes. "But duty's duty."

Willmore smiled.

"We can't have you goin' against your sense of duty, can we, uncle."

Stoner said: "Any sass to the sheriff

an' I'll knock your teeth down your throat. You ain't no kin of mine."

"Take it easy, Jake," Charlie said.

They lifted a lamp from the desk and took him to the cell. When they had pushed him inside they took the lamp away and he was left in darkness. He felt his way to the cot and lay full length on it. It looked like he was beaten.

He was very tired. He thought for a few minutes of the boys out at the camp and wondered what they would do now. He thought last of all about Helen Craytham before he fell into a deep sleep.

17

IT was dawn.

Old man Cary had been up an hour. He didn't believe in letting the young ones waste a minute of daylight when there was work to be done. He clanged noisily on his skillet with a ladle and yelled that if they didn't come and get it he'd throw it away. The boys had been working most of the night and had snatched no more than a few hours sleep. They decided unanimously to stop the night gathering for a while and to start on the branding. They had a good sized herd and it was felt generally that it was not a good thing that so many good cows were standing around without a brand on them. All of them had the Reeses in mind.

Tom Willmore was not back from town yet and that meant that he had been gone a day and two nights. They were all worried and one of them was going to ride into town today to find what had happened to him. Meanwhile by common consent Old Man Cary took charge. Today the branding would start and as Tom Willmore had decided, they would save hands and time by using a branding chute that he had devised in his head. He had described it in detail to them and there wasn't a man there who could not construct one to his specifications.

So the Old Man filled them up with a good breakfast and hot coffee and sent them on their way with stiff admonitions for them not to stand around, but to keep busy. The chute would be constructed to one side of the gate of the holding pen, one man would brand, one would feed him hot irons, two would bring him cows and the rest would hold the herd. And the Old Man would be over to see that they were doing things right when he had his Son-of-a-Bitch stew simmering nicely an' God help them if they didn't make that chute good and strong.

They caught up their horses and

departed. The two men on night herd came in for their breakfasts and he fed them. They ate, crawled thankfully into their blankets and knew they had only a few hours till the chute was finished and they were wanted again to hold the herd. The Old Man washed the dishes, put his stew, which he had prepared the day before on to simmer and caught up his old claybank gelding. He rode to the holding pen and found one of the Chavez boys and his sons at work on the branding chute. They were making a fair job of it and he didn't see why it shouldn't work. Save a hell of a lot of sweat and strain. It was new-fangled, but it was good. He rode back to his wagon and off-saddled. He was taking a sip of his stew from the ladel when the attack came.

The first thing he knew of it his large black kettle went *spaaaang* and sprung a leak through which his stew rapidly flowed.

Then a stutter of guns went off all around him and he was running for the wagon, yelling to the men in their blankets. They didn't know which way to go but stared around like owls. They were two of the Chavez boys.

He got his rifle from the wagon and was looking around for something to shoot at when the horsemen swept through the camp.

He threw up the rifle and fired as one of them thundered past him. The man heaved his horse around and he saw that it was big George Reese. Beyond him other horsemen were scattering out over the prairie, yelling and firing their guns. Another rider came through the camp, jumped his horse over the fire, knocked the kettle over and rode one of the Chavez boys down. The Mexican yelled shrilly.

George had a gun in his hand and he fired. He missed old Jim Cary and jumped his horse back toward him. The old rifle didn't hold any more than one shot and there was no time to put another round into the breech. With an obscene curse that would have curled the hair of a longhorn, the old man charged at the oncoming rider, swinging his rifle like a club.

He heard George laugh.

He tried to hit the man with his rifle, but George turned the horse aside cleverly, dodged the blow and then swung the animal back again. Its shoulder caught Cary in the side and bowled him over. He fell into the fire and roared. George nearly fell out of the saddle laughing.

He stopped laughing abruptly when one of the Chavez boys went for him with a knife. He managed to get in one painful slash at the man's leg, then George shot him through the chest and dropped him right alongside Old Man Cary.

George rode off then, swearing, heading for the rope corral with the remuda in it. He tore the rope down and scattered the horses, yelling at them and firing his gun in the air.

The Chavez boy who had been knocked down was weeping. He picked up the fallen rifle and begged Old Man Cary for ammunition so that he could shoot the gringo dog.

Old Jim Cary got groggily to his feet and went to the wagon. He found a box of ammunition, broke it open and filled his pockets. Then he went and took the rifle from the Mexican and loaded it. George Reese was riding away to join his fellows now.

Cary could see roughly what was going on out there. Horsemen seemed to be everywhere, firing from the saddle and yelling. Over by the holding pen, somebody was firing and several riders were swooping down on him. The rest were after the cattle, yelling and shooting. The whole bunch was running, heads down.

My God, Jim Cary suddenly realized, as terror washed through him, *they're coming this way*.

George Reese had already seen this. He turned his horse and was racing it across the oncoming tide of cattle. Dust rose from them in a choking cloud suddenly hiding the riders from the Old Man's view.

He fired at George and apparently missed because the man carried on in his wild dash for safety. Then Jim was shouting to the Mex to get to cover and was dragging the wounded one toward the wagon. The whole one helped him and they got the man to the comparative safety, but it looked to Jim a waste of time. The man seemed dead to him. It looked like the bullet had taken him clean through the heart.

The earth shook beneath them as the herd charged toward them. The Old Man looked at the wagon and he thought they didn't stand much chance. *What a way to die*, he thought. He looked at the Mexican and saw that the man looked as scared as he felt.

Jim grinned.

"Give me a hand," he said. "Turn the wagon over. That's our only chance."

They heaved together several times as the mass of cattle thundered toward them without managing to budge it. But finally with a superhuman effort they moved it, it swayed uncertainly and then went over with a crash. The noise of the cattle was now deafening.

They hit with a sound like two armed hosts coming together, wood splintered, a horn smashed through the woodwork of the wagon-bed. Cattle seemed to be clambering all over it. Something struck Jim on the temple and he went down. He fell on the Mexican and heard his yell of fear. He felt hot breath on his face and knew that he was a dead man.

When it was all over, the silence was like the silence of death.

Stunned, choking on dust and gunsmoke, Mose Green, walked wearily to his fallen horse and shot it through the head. Bill Cary who had taken cover in the holding pen behind the branding-chute walked out into the open, gun in hand, face grimed with gunsmoke. There was blood on his left shoulder. He was staring across the prairie in the direction of the wagon. He could barely see it as it lay on its side in the slowly settling dust. He looked around for his horse, feeling sick when he thought of what could have happened to his father.

The horses had taken off when the cattle had run. They were standing on the edge of the brush watching the men. One of the Chavez boys was running toward them with a rope in his hand.

Mose Green came near, loading his smoking gun.

"The bustards," he said. He too was glancing across to where the wagon lay, noting that there was no sign of movement over there.

After a few minutes, the Chavez boy caught up two horses and came loping toward them, leading one. Bill Cary caught it. His brother Jed came from the other end of the pen, running, out of breath.

"The Wagon," he said.

Bill said: "The cows hit it."

He rode off with Chavez following him. Green and Jed ran after them awkward on their high heels.

When they finally panted up to what was left of the wagon they found Bill standing still staring down at his father. A glance was enough to tell them what a cow's hoof had done to the Old Man's head. Jed's strong young body shuddered violently.

The Chavez boy who had ridden ahead with Bill was holding his dead brother in his arms and was weeping violently. The other one who had been behind the wagon with Jim Cary lay on the ground moaning.

Bill turned and looked at his brother. Their eyes met in silent and despairing communication. They didn't speak. Everybody stayed just where they were, stunned.

Brush crashed as horsemen approached the camp from the east.

Mose Green pulled his Dragoon from leather and cocked it. Bill took a quick stride to his horse and yanked his carbine from its boot. Two riders came into view. It was Miguel Chavez followed by Sam Cary. As soon as they rode up and piled from the saddle the others saw that they did not know of the two deaths. Their eyes terrible, they gazed down on the Old Man with his head trodden in and the

Mexican with the blood caking in the heat on his chest.

Miguel crossed himself.

Sam said: "Oh, my God."

Finally Bill said: "Just standin' here won't help none." But nobody made a move but Mose Green who found a spade among the wreckage and started digging. After a while Miguel pulled himself together and found a tool also and joined him. When they had exhausted themselves in the hard ground two others took over. When the graves were dug, they put the two men in them side by side. Then the Mexicans prayed and the Texans stood silent as they threw the first handfuls of dirt on the dead men. After that they finished the job with the shovels and patted the red soil down neatly.

The rest stood or sat around, not knowing what to do while Sam told the others that he and Miguel had gone after the cattle and had run into a strong ambush a mile or so to the east. They had been lucky to get out of that alive. Mose Green started to salvage what he could from the wreckage. He found some cans of tomatoes in Jim's store and handed them around. The men bust them open with their knives and drank the refreshing contents. Then Mose borrowed Sam's horse and went after the horses. He caught three or four, came back and saddled a bay.

"I'm goin' into town to get Tom," he said. "He'll know what to do."

"There ain't nothin' to do," Bill Cary said. "We're finished."

Miguel lifted his head.

"This happens to us and the patron does not come back from town," he said. "Mose is right. Something could have happened to him. More than one should go maybe."

Mose said: "I'll handle this alone." He said it in a way that didn't brook opposition. They looked at him listlessly and let him go.

When Mose reached town it was dark. He left his horse on the edge of Mex town and walked across the bridge. He wasn't furtive, but he didn't advertise himself either. He walked straight past the sheriff's office, noted that there was a light inside and went right on to Mary Willmore's house.

There was no light showing at the front, so he walked around the rear. There was a light in the kitchen. He rapped on the door with the butt of his quirt and the girl's voice called out: "Who's this?"

"Mose Green, ma'am."

The door opened and the girl stared at him wide-eyed.

"You know me, ma'am." She nodded. "Miz Willmore's tophand. I'm a lookin' for him, ma'am." He wondered if he was frightening her, a battered black man standing there in the half-light, more horse than man and knowing it. She looked a little scared sure enough.

"They arrested him, Mose," she said.

"They got him in the jail here?"

She nodded.

He said: "Thank you kindly, ma'am," and started to turn away.

"Just a minute," she said. He stopped and looked back at her, rolling his eyes so the whites showed. "What're you going to do?"

"Do?" he said, his face graven. "Why I aim to bust him out, ma'am." He walked on.

She wanted to stop him, to tell him that he would only make matters worse for Willmore, but there was something about him that was implacable and she knew that she could not stop him.

He walked around the house, onto the street and went straight to the sheriff's office. He felt nothing, no fear or apprehension, and only knew his intent that Willmore should be free. There was no doubt in his simple and direct mind that he could do what he intended.

He opened the door to the office and walked in shutting the door behind him and putting his back against it.

The sheriff was at his desk with a bottle of whiskey in front of him. The deputy sat at another desk playing solo. They looked at him, distaste showing on their faces.

"There's been two killin's," he said.

The sheriff jumped to his feet and the deputy showed surprise.

"Two killings!" the sheriff exclaimed.

"They killed Old Man Cary and Pedro Chavez."

"Who's they?"

"The Reeses."

Stoner tossed down a card and stood up.

"Now, see here, nigger," he said.

Mose stared at him unblinkingly and drew the Dragoon. The sound of it cocking was very loud in the stillness of the room.

"You be still and hush your mouth," he said. "White trash."

He enjoyed seeing the white man shake with a sudden burst of rage that was held in check by the sight of the big gun.

The sheriff started to say something, but he stammered badly and at first it wouldn't come out. Then he managed in as gruff and manly a voice as he could summon to say: "Now stop this foolish-ness. Put that gun away."

Mose looked at him blandly.

"Mister," he said, "this foolishness ain't even begun. You, turn around."

The deputy looked as if he would have liked to refuse, but he looked at the gun and turned around. Mose walked slowly across the room. He reached out for the sheriff's gun where it lay on the desk and tossed it into the corner. Then he walked up to Stoner and hit him hard over the head with the heavy barrel of the Dragoon. The man let out a moan and fell to the floor. Mose stepped back and gazed down at him. He didn't smile, but he said: "I sure 'nough liked doin' that." He turned to the shaking sheriff. "Old man, you do jest like I say or I bust your head for you-all. Git in there an' let Miz Willmore out."

"You fool—" the sheriff began.

Mose moved up close to him and jammed his gun in the spreading midriff.

"Move," he said, "an' save the words."

Charlie Willmore moved. He found his

key-ring on a hook, lifted a lamp from the desk and went through the side door to the cells. Mose followed. As he entered the cell area, he called: "Tom, boy, where's you at?"

The lamplight fell on Willmore coming up to the bars. He looked amazed at the sight of the Negro.

"For God's sake, Mose," he said.

"Now don't you start arguin'," Mose said. "I heard enough talk already. You're goin' outa here before they hang you."

The sheriff rattled a key into the lock and the door swung open.

Willmore said: "This could mean real trouble for you, Mose."

"Trouble," Mose said. "I got more trouble than I can handle. That's why I'm bustin' you-all outa here. The Reese's done killed Pedro Chavez and Ol' Man Cary dead."

"You mean—"

"They jumped us. They done scattered all our cows an' hosses. They sure 'nough played hell."

Willmore stayed still a moment as that

208

sank in. Then he moved. He took hold of the sheriff and pushed him into the cell.

"Lie down on the bed," he said.

The sheriff started to protest, but Willmore pushed him down on the bed, took off his bandanna and gagged him with it. Charlie Willmore spluttered a lot but it didn't do him any good. Mose Green went out into the office and started to look after the deputy. Willmore took off the sheriff's belt and strapped his ankles together. His wrists he bound behind him with strips taken from a blanket. He left the sheriff in the dark, trying to say something, trying to plead or curse, and walked into the office where the Negro had Stoner trussed up like a fowl. The man was just coming around to conscious and looked terrible. There was blood down the side of his face and murder in his eyes.

Mose said: "Help me carry him into the cells."

They carried him between them and dumped him in the cell with the sheriff. They were making muffled sounds as the two men hurried back into the office to find Willmore's gun in the sheriff's drawer. He strapped it on and that made him feel a whole lot better. He headed for the door, but Green stopped him.

"Out the rear."

"Where your horses?"

"Edge of Mex town."

"I have a horse back in the brush. Been there nearly a couple of days. Ride down the creek and meet me at the old ford. You know it?"

"Sure."

"Right, you go by the street, I'll slip out back." Mose turned toward the door. "Mose."

"Yes?"

"Thanks."

"You're purely welcome."

They parted, Mose walking carelessly onto the street not looking to right or left, Willmore going quietly out the back.

He walked for about thirty minutes and that gave him time to think. Time to think about Old Jim Cary and Pedro Chavez. Both good men in their own ways. It had been Cary's kind who had made Texas. The salt of the earth. And they came none better than Chavez. A poor man and born to hardship, he had been honest and honorable in his own light. He had survived in a hard world and been respected by his fellows. A man could not ask for more than that.

So what lay before Willmore now? He didn't know any of the details, but he knew that his cows were scattered and there had been two more men killed. That meant a lot of hard work to be done all over again and it had to be done in constant danger from the Reese's guns. It also meant that by the code of the country Willmore had an even bigger debt to pay. This was something the law would not or could not look after for him. His brother Bart, Jim Cary and Pedro Chavez—they all had to be paid for. The world would expect it of him. He would demand it of himself.

He found the sorrel hungry and thirsty, gnawing at the bark of a tree, every mesquite bean within reach eaten. It whinnied joyfully at the sight of him. He stroked its velvet muzzle, untied it and mounted. It let him take it to the water at a swift trot and there it started taking on water. A horse doesn't have the sense of a mule with water and doesn't know when to stop, so Willmore let it have just so much and no more, before he heaved its head up and took it across the ford.

Mose Green appeared, riding one horse and leading another. Willmore changed his saddle from the sorrel to the fresh horse. Mounted, he led the way at a brisk trot, savoring the night, refreshed already in the clean air after the musty closeness of the jail.

After thirty minutes, Willmore swung left along a smaller side-trail. Mose caught up with him and said: "This ain't the way to camps, boy."

"It's the way to the Craytham place."

"Sure, I know that."

"That's where we're going."

Mose wanted to say that this was no time for courting, but he held his tongue. He was so glad to have Willmore out of jail that he reckoned he'd go along with anything he did.

Within the hour, they rode into the Craytham's yard and hailed the house. There was a short pause before a light showed and the woman came out onto the stoop. Willmore called to her, dismounted and went toward her. Mose couldn't see much what went on in the moon-shadow of the stoop, but he reckoned he saw Willmore take the woman's hands in his. They talked for maybe five minutes and the Negro didn't hear a word. But finally the man patted the woman's arm and came back to his horse. He lifted his hand in farewell and Mrs. Craytham returned the salute and then they were once more riding down the trail in the moonlight.

"Wastin' time," Mose muttered.

Willmore was curt with him.

"You think I'm damn fool enough to waste time at a time like this, you should of left me in jail."

They didn't draw rein till shortly after dawn when they rode into the remains of the cow-camp on tired horses.

Everybody there greeted them with guns in their hands. Not much was said and they ate a cold and miserable breakfast. Willmore was tired and said that he was going to get some sleep.

Bill Cary said: "Hell, this ain't no time for sleep. What're we goin' to do, Tom?"

"Give me two hours in my blankets."

"We're wastin' time."

"Then catch cows."

"I had in mind a killin' or two. That's my old man in that grave there."

Willmore squatting on his heels looked up at the big man. "That's my friend and one of my riders there. My brother's also dead."

"I didn't mean . . ."

"There're two things we have to do and we have to get our priorities right. Without cows we're finished and I don't aim to be finished. People depend on us. I'm trailing a herd north. You go catch cows, Bill, an' brand 'em as fast as you bring 'em in."

"Yes, but—"

"An' you brand 'em," Willmore picked

up a stick and drew in the dust, "with this."

Jed Cary said: "Christ, that's—"

"We all know what it is," Willmore said. "That's how we brand 'em. I'm an outlaw. The Flying W's outlawed. You have a new owner. If you have sense you won't use the Cary brand either or you'll make it over to cover the cows that still carry it."

Sam Cary said: "Jumpin' snakes, he's right."

Miguel Chavez nodded his ugly head.

"You are right, patron. First, the cows and then . . . the men."

They all nodded, agreeing.

Willmore and Mose turned into their blankets and fell almost instantly asleep to the sound of the others catching up their horses and riding off into the brush.

18

THEY had never seen Morgan Reese in such a rage. The usually cool and collected man was beside himself. Clancy had ridden out from town with the news of Willmore's escape and the sheriff's humiliation. They sat around on the gallery of the big house and they talked, all the men of the clan: Morgan raging; Clancy irritable and half-guilty as though he were to blame for the turn of events; Regan coldly promising himself that if Willmore didn't hang he would die by his, Regan's gun; Bull smoldering angrily like the bull he was; Loge, Henry and George waiting for the decision to be made for them so they could saddle up and act.

"My God, Morg," Clancy said, spilling the whiskey in his glass in his agitation, "you can't blame me. I took him. I shut him up in that jail. If that fool of a sheriff can't—"

"God damn it," Morgan shouted, "nobody's blaming you. Shut up and let me think. First, that dim-wit Charlie Willmore must go."

"That won't put Willmore back in jail," Bull said, not unpleased to goad Morgan whose brains he resented.

"You put your two cents worth in when you're asked," Morgan snapped. "We have to have a plan of action. Now, what will Willmore do now he's out?"

"Come a-gunning for us," Loge said.

Morgan jerked his head around to him, birdlike and sharp. "Will he, though? He's no fool. He wants a herd to take north. He's going to be occupied in catching cows."

Bull laughed.

"We'll uncatch 'em for him as fast as he does."

Morgan frowned, thinking.

"There're more ways of killing a coyote than by hanging," he said, cooling suddenly and smiling as the ideas started coming to him. "Now let's weigh the chances. As fighting men, he has only the Cary boys. The Mexes don't count. They're good with cattle but that's about all. The Carys're going to have their hands full of cows."

"Look," Regan interrupted, "why we so all-fired keen on taking their cows. Don't we have enough of our own."

"Listen to the man," Morgan shouted, some of his rage showing itself again. "We have maybe seven hundred, a thousand cows to call our own. How far's that going with our family our size. I'll tell you, we're taking north the biggest herd Kansas ever saw. They'll talk about the Reeses and their drive when the longhorn's forgotten. We go north with three-four thousand cows. Two herds if we have to."

"Sure," Bull said. "That's the talk I like to hear. I ain't content with pea-nuts even if Regan is. Think big, act big, that's me."

"Talk big," Regan said.

"Why, you—"

"Order," Morgan bellowed. "God damn you, order."

Clancy said: "So we're still after the cows. But the Willmore's aren't the only cows in the country. There's the Nevinson's and the Brown's. I hold notes on both their places at the bank. I can finish 'em tomorrow."

"I'm coming to that," Morgan said. "You go ahead with that, Clance. Get that fool sheriff onto it. But first we have him raise a posse and go after Willmore."

Loge said: "Where'll you raise a posse in this man's country to take a Willmore?"

Morgan looked at him aghast.

"Don't talk that way. The man's an outlaw. He's broken jail. The sheriff *has* to raise a posse. If he can't pull it off that way, by God, we'll bring the nigger cavalry in. Don't forget I have the governor's ear. He don't have no time for Johnny Rebs and that's what Willmore still is. We'll finish his hashin' no time at all. Meanwhile, I have another plan.

Didn't you tell me, Regan, that he was sparking poor Craytham's widow?"

Regan laughed.

"What've you thought up, you old rogue, you?" he asked.

Morgan leaned forward conspiratorially. "Just you listen to this."

19

TO those who do not know the brush country of south-west Texas, it could have seemed like madness for Willmore to have broken jail and gone straight back to catching cows. But he knew it and knew that he was comparatively safe from the law in the wild entanglement of the brasada. Safe that is, so long as he did not meet with treachery.

He carried on much as before, riding and roping with the men, recklessly riding the thickets, catching up the cows that the Reeses had lost them, gathering in some that had never known the rope before. But he lived with an increased wariness, for now he knew that he must fear the law as well as the Reeses. Charlie Willmore had now come out in the open and shown himself to be a tool of the powerful clan.

In the week that followed the bunch in

the holding pen steadily grew. The new branding chute proved a success. They were branding cows, or so big Bill Cary declared, as fast as the damned buckaroos could catch 'em. They were busy with the cattle, but Willmore did not altogether neglect to watch the Reeses. He sent Mose Green as the best man for sign after the party of men who had raided the camp and found that they had taken with them as many as three hundred head of a mixed bunch. All unbranded. And Willmore knew that no sooner did he have a fair-sized herd together than the Reeses would be back. These men were revengeful and cattle-hungry. The two things together made them something to reckon with.

A week to the day, the Nevinsons rode in. They were Seth Nevinson a small wiry man in his middle years, his son John and two riders. They were old neighbours of the Carys and the Willmores. Willmore had known them all his life. They brought the news that after the Reeses had mavericked for weeks through the

222

Nevinson herds, they had now foreclosed on the home place through the bank. The Nevinsons were finished. Seth added that Marty Brown was in the same boat and would also be coming over to see Willmore. The Reeses were sure riding high and they looked too tough to bring down.

Most of the men were out after cows. It was noon and Willmore sat talking with the disconsolate men, eating hard tack and washing it down with bitter coffee. He welcomed Seth and his crew, not only because they were neighbours and neighbours should stick together, but because they were hands and God knew he needed them desperately. He made his offer straight away, the same that he had made to the Carys and Chavez. Come in on the drive for shares.

"And who knows," he said with a smile, "by the time this ends there may be a few hundred Reese mavericks in our bunch."

Miguel Chavez came riding in from the south. His horse was lathered and he was excited. He slid to the ground and ran to Willmore, crying out: "Patron, your uncle comes. With him are many men."

Seth Nevinson said: "Time for you to disappear, Tom. Go on, we'll hold him off."

Willmore did not waste any time. He ran to his already saddled horse and stepped into the saddle. He rode off into the north and joined the small crew that were combing the thickets there.

Within five minutes of his departure Charlie Willmore rode onto the prairie backed by his deputy, wearing a bandage under his hat, and ten men. Stoner looked sick and mad, the sheriff looked nervous.

The riders halted and sat their saddles, staring at the men gathered near the fire. There were no greetings offered back to Charlie Willmore when he said: "Howdy."

Bill Cary said coldly: "What do you want, Willmore?"

"I come for Tom, Bill," the sheriff said, "an' mean to have him."

Stoner said: "An' Green. I mean to have *him*."

"You won't find either here."

"This is murder, Bill. I mean business."

Bill Cary stood up.

"There's two graves over yonder," he said. "In one's my daddy, in the other's Pedro Chavez. How about *them?*"

"I only just had the news. I'm lookin' into that now. I promise you somebody'll pay for that. I'm not takin' sides. There's goin' to be law in this country."

Bill laughed bitterly.

"While you're at it get our cows back from the Reeses."

"You bringin' a charge against them?"

Bill Cary cut the air with the edge of his hand. "Cut it out, Charlie. You know as well as we do this is a farce. You ain't goin' to catch no murderers. You know any man from around here will hide Tom for killing a Reese."

Stoner kneed his horse forward.

"This bastard wants coolin' off," he said, "an' I'm the man to do it."

Quickly, Charlie said: "Leave it, Jake."

Seth Nevinson pulled his holster forward onto his thigh. "Take your boys outa here, Willmore," he said. "It could be a massacre."

"I don't have to take that kind of talk," the sheriff said. "An' while you're here, Nevinson, you may as well hear that the bank's forclosin' on your place."

The Nevinsons and their two men gazed at him in silence.

Seth stood up, facing the sheriff and the posse squarely.

"You'll need the Bluecoats, sheriff," he said. "Best go get 'em before you get hurt."

Stoner dropped his hand to his gunbutt and the sheriff said in a sharp high-pitched tone: "No!" His horse jumped sideways and blocked the way between the deputy and the rancher. "You tell my nephew when he comes in to stop playin' the fool and give himself up. I want that nigger too for bustin' him out. You got that clear."

Bill Cary said: "You want 'em, you find 'em."

Charlie said: "Aaaah!" in disgust and wheeled his horse away. Stoner stayed a moment, staring belligerently at the men below him, but he too thought better of it and went after his superior. The posse followed slowly behind. They rode off into the east and were quickly lost to view in the brush.

The whole crew were working on the herd and the branding chute when Tom Willmore returned an hour later. The Nevinsons and their two riders were there. He drew Seth aside and they talked. Seth had decided to throw in with them. Willmore discussed with him how the work should go and told him that he was going riding. He would be gone about a day.

"What do you aim on doin'?" the man asked suspiciously.

"Best you don't know, Seth. Let's say the Reeses have to be slowed up for a while or they'll hit us again. I aim to slow 'em up. We don't have enough hands to spare for a shootin' war. We need us a herd. You, the Carys and the Chavez see that we get it an' I'll attend to the kind of work I know."

Seth said: "Hell, Tom, don't be a damn fool. You can't go against the Reeses on your lonesome."

"You think of the herd and nothin' else."

"I don't like it."

"Nobody asked you to, you old fool."

Seth smiled wryly and held out his hand.

"Luck, any road," he said.

They shook.

Willmore turned away, rode his tired bay to the remuda and roped the young sorrel. He was going to need a horse with a turn of speed. He threw the saddle on the colt and rode off into the east in the direction taken by the posse.

A short while after, Mose Green rode in from the west and learned of the arrival of the posse from Bill Cary.

"Where's Tom?" the Negro asked.

Bill put down the branding iron he was

holding. "Maybe Seth knows. Hey, Seth, where did Tom go?"

Seth Nevinson loped his roan over and said: "I reckon he went to war."

Mose and Bill looked at each other.

Bill said: "Hell's bells, why didn't he tell us? He can't do nothin' on his lonesome."

"That's what I told him." Seth said. "But he said it was more important we stay with the herd."

Bill was angry.

"He wants it all for himself. God damn! He knows damn well we Carys . . ."

Mose said: "He's right. We gotta have the cows. Well, you hombres don't need an ol' nigger man around. Reckon I'll mosey along and see what the chile's doin'."

"I'll come, Mose," Bill said.

Seth said: "No, you stay put, Bill. You should too, Mose. We need every hand we can muster."

Mose glowered fiercely.

"Young Tom's my boss," he said and turned his fleabitten mustang away. He loped hard for the remuda, caught up a black gelding and threw his hull on it. A few minutes later, he was trotting his way east.

20

IT was quiet at the Reese place except for the sound of the cicadas and the soft singing of one of the Mexican hands in the bunk-house.

Morgan and his clan were drinking whiskey on the front gallery. They had had a hard day and were visibly enjoying the luxury of lounging there, drinking and idly talking. There was a sense of well-being in every man. Things would go their way from now on. They reckoned it didn't make much odds that Tom Willmore was now free. His hash would be settled very shortly now.

Suddenly, Loge, the youngest and the one with the sharpest ears sat up straight and said: "Listen."

Morgan, who was doing the talking as usual stopped and frowned. He did not like to be interrupted when he was in full spate.

"What is it?" he demanded.

"Rider coming. And he's sure raising the dust."

They all listened and after the passage of a minute, they heard the rapid drumming of horses' hoofs. One or two of them rose and stepped down into the yard. The horseman swept off the road and pounded onto the hardened earth of the yard. He brought his animal to a skidding halt and dropped from the saddle. By the light of the lamps on the gallery, they saw that it was Ellson Roberts one of their top-hands. He had been with the southern herd.

Bull, the nearest to him, caught him by the arm.

"What in hell's up?" he demanded.

The man turned a sweat and dust-caked face to him. There was a streak of blood across one cheek.

"They hit the herd."

Morgan came stamping down the steps. "Who did?"

"God knows, Mr. Reese. It was as dark as hell. They come out of the night.

Before we knew what had happened there was fire among the cows. I don't know. I just don't know."

He was seized by the anguish of a good cowman who's lost his gather. His eyes were wild and his words came babbling out.

"Pull yourself together, man," Morgan roared and shook the tough figure of the top-hand.

With Morgan and Bull on either side of him, Loge stepped forward to face him.

"Who were they?"

"I didn't see a damn one of them. All I know is there was a lot of shooting, some of us got hit and the cows were runnin'. Christ, they must be scattered over half Texas by now."

There was a lot more of it, but Morgan cut him short with a curt: "Shut up, I've heard enough." Men were running from the bunk-house. The Mexican song had stopped abruptly. Morgan glared around at them all. Morgan went on: "Every man mounted. Loge, spare horses for every man. Every God-damned Reese rides tonight. Even you, Regan. Come dawn I want every man after that herd. Morales, you ride with a message from me to the sheriff. If this is Willmore's work we'll soon have him back in jail."

Regan said, grinning: "Keep your shirt on, Morg. We have the hole card. Tomorrow Willmore should know his hands're tied."

Morgan didn't seem to hear. He was turned and climbing the gallery steps, striding into the house, roaring for his Negro servant, yelling for his guns.

The men scattered, the Reeses bawling orders. Within thirty minutes, the whole small army of men were gathered, armed and prepared, standing by their horses with the remuda moving uneasily under the two wranglers beyond the edge of the light. Morgan's wife and Loge's came out onto the gallery and both women looked scared. Morgan came hurrying out of the house and snatched the lines from the hands of his servant. The man boosted him into the saddle. He led the way out of the yard at a brisk trot. His army followed behind. In all their minds were the cattle. Their main stake for the future. Their minds were now concentrated on regaining them.

Roberts rode by Morgan's side. When they had gone along the road for a half-mile, he yelled that they had reached the cut off and swerved through the screen of mesquite and led the way into the south-east. The cavalcade thundered at his heels. They drove through the mesquite for another couple of miles and came into broken country. The stars were bright now and they could see an eerie landscape in the pale light. Of necessity, their pace slowed; hoofs clinked on rock and now and then a horse stumbled. There was no sound except for the echo of hoofs, the creak of saddle-leather and the music of bridle-chains. Roberts led the way up a dry-wash.

They were halfway down it when the shot came.

Nobody knew who or if anybody was hit, but a horse in the centre of the bunch of riders reared with a shrill neigh. That seemed a signal for all the horses to lose their heads and for a moment it seemed that every man there put his attention on his mount.

Before they had their animals under proper control a second and third shot rang out.

Now a horse lunged forward and went down. The wranglers started yelling excitedly as the remuda which was bringing up the rear lost its nerve and some of its members tried scaling the walls of the arroyo.

Somebody pulled a gun and started firing at the rocks above and every man there did his best to scatter, while every Reese there bawled orders.

Bull lost his horse in the first few seconds and was hurled to the ground where he lay half-stunned. Morgan with Regan and Roberts in the lead, spurred ahead and in seconds were out of the fight. Some men in the rear went after the remuda which now turned in on itself and fled back the way it had come. Mulford tumbled from the saddle with lead in his shoulder, Henry had his arm grazed, before men had time to dismount from their horses and get into the cover of the rocks. When they turned at bay here, guns in their hands, there was no more shooting. They crouched there behind the cover of rock listening to the silence of the night that was broken only by the sound of the fleeing cavvy.

They waited, staring this way and that, as the horses moved restlessly on the bed of the drywash.

After five minutes in which no man found the courage to come out from cover and for which nobody blamed him, there came the sound of horses above them. Each man listened carefully to interpret the sounds, each man knew that there was no more than two horsemen riding away into the night.

Bull heaved himself up from the sand of the river-bed, anger choking him.

"Two of 'em," he said. "An' there's more'n a dozen cringin' here like they was attacked by an army."

Men started to come out from cover.

Morgan, Regan and Roberts came riding back. If Bull was angry, then Morgan was beside himself. He ordered Bull to go after the men with the remuda and to come on to the cow-camp. He was going ahead. By God, Willmore would pay for this. Somebody was bold enough to ask how he knew it was Willmore.

"Who else do you think it was, you God-damned fool?" was the furious reply.

"What about the wounded?" Regan asked. He was sensitive about wounds, because his own slight wound was still sore.

"Who's hurt?"

They all looked at each other. Mulford came forward, bent shouldered, holding one arm.

"I got it in the shoulder."

"Bad?"

Mulford wasn't the kind of man to admit pain. "I'll live," he said. "I'll live to plant the bastard that did this."

"Any more?"

One of the vaqueros had turned an ankle jumping from his horse. An Anglo

238

cowhand had his foot trodden on by a horse. Henry had his arm grazed. Morgan declared that all the injured but Henry could go back to the house and have the women look at them. Henry was a Reese. Let somebody patch him up and he could spend the next day catching cows like anybody else. Somebody at the back of the bunch of men swore that Morgan was a hard-hearted son-of-a-bitch.

Morgan mounted and said for God's sake let's get on, this wasn't a catastrophe. He'd have Willmore behind bars before very long now and pretty soon he'd be dangling by his neck. There was going to be law around here.

They all climbed onto their animals. Morgan led the majority off towards the cow-camp, the injured straggled slowly home.

They had hunted cows for a day when a rider came from the house to say that somebody had set fire to the bunk-house and barn and they were burned to the ground. There were two more wounded and every horse in the place had been scattered. The women were terrified and Mrs. Morgan had demanded that Morgan come home where he belonged. Morgan who had never received such a message from his wife in all his life was flabbergasted. Rage seemed to be a commonplace with him these days. The cool cold-thinking man seemed to have gone forever. He held a council-of-war with his clan. They were all tired from chasing cows in impenetrable thickets and depressed by the news from the vaqueros that several hundred of their unbranded stock had been driven west.

Morgan told the others: "This *must* be Willmore's doing. I know for sure that the Craytham kids headed for his camp. They must have taken news their mother was taken. If Willmore knows that he wouldn't be raising hell."

"Maybe he does know. In which case this isn't him. Maybe it's the Carys or the Nevinsons. They both owe us something."

"They don't have the guts."

"Don't be so damned sure," Bull said. "They're all fighting men."

Morgan snarled: "You put your mind to catching cows and leave them to me."

He took Regan and Loge with him and rode off toward home to see what the damage was. He was confused. He wasn't used to things not going his way. His hatred of Willmore was deeper than ever.

21

WILLMORE and Mose Green rode steadily into the west. They were tired with the tiredness of a job well done. They both knew that they had held the Reeses for a good few days now. They weren't exactly triumphant, because neither of them were fools and both knew that the unexpected could face them at any moment. But they felt their spirits lift after their late defeats.

Neither of them had suffered a scratch during the two days and nights they had been busy on Reese land. In that time they had scattered the trail herd, heading a substantial part of it into the west where they could be picked up by their own riders; they had scattered the horse-herd —which was fairly easily catchable, but which would hold the Reeses up when they didn't have time to spare. They had fired the barn and the bunk-house. More than that. After the women had taken themselves into town where they would be safe from the danger they thought threatened them, the two of them shot up the house while Morgan, Loge and Regan were in it. The men put up a fight, but Willmore and Green had no intention of fighting.

They rode away, leaving a deeply disturbed leader and two bewildered followers with most of the windows of their home shot in, a whole lot of china broken and their morale as low as it had ever been.

Not having taken more than cat-naps in two days, Willmore and Mose now rode slowly back to camp on equally tired horses.

They found half the crew at the branding chute with Bill Cary in charge of them. Here also to Willmore's astonishment, they found the two Craytham boys. At the sight of them a thrill went through Willmore and he looked around at once for their mother. At sight of him the two boys climbed down from their perches on

243

the corral fence and came toward him. Bill Cary came with them, an arm around their shoulders. Something about the boys' faces told Willmore that something was wrong. He swung from the saddle.

"Hello, boys," he said. "You bring your ma with you?"

They didn't say anything, but the little one's lower lip quivered.

Bill Cary said: "A hell of a note, Tom."

Sudden fear swooped in Willmore's belly.

"What happened?"

"They took Mrs. Craytham."

The other men were stopping work and coming toward them, the dust caked to their sweat. Miguel Chavez was there.

Willmore stood very still looking at Bill Cary and the boys, almost unable to believe what he had heard. Things like that didn't happen to women in this country.

"Jimmy," he said, "what happened?"

The elder boy said, "Regan Reese came. He put Sam an' me on our ponies and told us where to come to find you.

We was to tell you that he had took our ma."

"That all?"

"He said if you want her, you come an' get her."

"I didn't know what to do, Tom," Bill Cary said. "Christ, I know I should ought to have gotten the boys together and jumped the whole dirty bunch of 'em. But there was Mrs. Craytham . . ."

Willmore said: "There wasn't anything you could do."

He turned and walked away to the wagon. Mose Green followed him leading the horses. There was coffee in the pot. They built the fire up and heated the coffee, sat silently drinking it and smoking. The men went back to their work. The boys perched themselves on the fence again. Acrid smoke rose from the branded hides, cows lowed for their calves.

Finally, Mose said: "This is bad, boy. They got us hamstrung."

Willmore looked at him morosely, saying nothing. It came home to him just what the woman meant to him. Just as strongly it came home to him what he meant to do.

At last he rose and said: "Mose, you catch up on your sleep."

"What're you goin' to do?"

"I'm doin' it alone."

"Now see here—"

Angrily, Willmore said: "Don't give me no God-damned argument."

Mose looked hurt and went to say something, but Willmore walked away toward the holding pen. Here, he told Bill Cary: "Get the two boys to work. They can help young Chavez with the horses."

Bill said: "They ain't no more'n kids."

"I was catchin' cows with my old man at their age. Keep 'em busy."

"What you aim to do, Tom?"

"Get Mrs. Craytham back."

"You'll need all hands for the cows."

He slapped Bill on the shoulder and the big man watched him tramping back to the wagon. *My God,* Cary thought, *the man's bushed. What does he hope to do like that.*

Willmore caught up his strongest horse, a dun, then dropped his loop over a mettlesome little roan. He saddled the dun, ignoring Mose's watchful eyes, then went to the wagon. From there he filled his pockets with ammunition for the rifle and gun. That done, he went to Mose lying in his blankets and said: "This time you don't follow me, Mose."

"No, sir," Mose said and turned over to sleep.

Willmore walked to the dun, mounted and rode off leading the roan.

Mose rose on one elbow and looked after him. "Damn fool obstinate like his old man," he said with some pride. "Now sleep for this chile."

Willmore left the horses deep in the mesquite at what he reckoned was a quarter mile from the house. He did not know if Regan was here, but he had to start somewhere. If not with Regan with somebody else. All he knew was that the thought of Helen in the hands of these men was insufferable and that he had to

247

keep moving. In spite of the tiredness that soaked clear through to his bones, action was the only antedote for his emotions.

He tramped through the brush, his senses alert. He had with him only a pistol and knife for weapons. For what he was about to do called for close work and his rifle wasn't needed.

Shortly, he came to the edge of the yard and viewed the house in the moonlight. It stood stark with the burned out barn and bunkhouse flanking it. There was a light burning on the ground floor and one above. Somebody sat on the gallery smoking a cigar.

Willmore worked his way around the house, keeping well in the shadows. There was a lamp alight in a lower room. Going in closer he saw that it was two Mexican women at work in a kitchen. He was starting to work his way around to the front of the house when he was startled by the sound of approaching horses. Crouching down at the edge of the starve-out, he saw a body of horsemen sweep into the yard. The moonlight glittered on weapons and metal buckles. Their faces gleamed darkly. They were Negro cavalry led by a white officer. With him even at this distance Willmore could see Loge Reese.

Both whitemen dismounted. A Negro sergeant leaned from the saddle to hold their lines. The two men walked up onto the gallery. The figure sitting there rose to meet them, first turning up a lamp that stood on a table. Willmore saw that it was Morgan Reese.

He heard the murmur of their voices, but could not make out what they were saying. After they had talked a short while, the officer shouted something to the sergeant who gave the order to dismount. The men swung from their saddles. Morgan shouted something and a man hurried from the house and led the sergeant and his men away.

Willmore bellied down and Indianed his way toward the house, but he had no sooner got under the lea of the gallery than the men moved inside.

He lay there thinking furiously,

wondering how the hell he could get Regan away from the others.

Then the dog found him.

He was unaware of it until it sniffed and growled almost in his ear. He batted its head away from him, rolling over on one elbow and the animal backed off snarling. Willmore's hand dropped to the butt of his gun as the first bark came. The animal yelped and jumped away as he swung the heavy weapon and took a swipe at it. But it at once regained its courage and ran in, teeth bared, growling fiercely.

Willmore swore venemously and rose to one knee, tempted to shoot the beast and knowing that he dared not. The animal started to make an awful racket, dancing around him, alternately snarling and barking.

Heavy footsteps drummed on the planks overhead and somebody shouted: "What in hell's going on there?"

The dog leapt in and Willmore guarded his throat from its fangs with his forearm. He managed to get a foot under the animal and booted it away. It hit the ground on its side, scrambled to its feet and leapt into the attack again.

A man jumped from the gallery into the yard and Willmore glimpsed him, gun in hand. Willmore rolled into deeper shadow and found himself under the house itself. Cautiously, he began to crawl.

"Something under the house," a man shouted. "Go on, boy, get 'im out."

The dog needed no second bidding, but came scrambling after Willmore. This time Willmore swung the gun with some effect. He caught the dog with the barrel on the head and sent it howling. He glared around and saw a man crouched down, peering into the darkness under the house. Willmore started worming his way toward the rear of the house.

A minute passed. He paused to look around and get his bearings. From not ten feet away, he clearly heard a man say: "There's a man under there, Morg. This dog's been hit with a gun-barrel."

Another voice said: "Hold him there,

Mr. Reese. I'll get my men. We'll soon flush him out of there."

Footsteps pounded as a man ran off. He heard the white officer calling for his sergeant.

He had to get out of there damned fast. He'd have to forget what he came for. He'd be lucky to get out of this alive.

He saw a pair of legs in front of him. Twelve paces to the left was another pair. He angled away from them, crawling as silently as he knew how.

Boots scuffed in the dust and the music of spurs came to him. He reached the rear of the house and was met by those self-same boots. He swore silently. Looking around he reckoned that, as far as he could be sure, he and the boots were alone at the rear of the house. Using elbows and knees he got to the edge of the building and peered out and up.

A man stood with his back half-turned to him.

It was now or never. He might get away with it, he might get a shot in the back from a man he could not see.

He raised himself on his elbows and cocked his gun.

At the faint sound, the man began to turn.

"Stay still," Willmore said, "or you're dead."

The man froze.

Willmore got slowly to his feet. He reached forward and lifted the gun from leather.

"Turn around," he said.

The man turned.

It was Regan Reese. Maybe there was a thin slice of luck here.

"Walk away from the house, Regan. Move a hand, even sniff loud and I'll shoot. My nerves're actin' up somethin' awful."

Regan looked at him.

"You're crazy," he said. "Drop that gun and don't be a fool. This place is crawling with soldiers. You won't get a yard."

"Move," Willmore said. He thrust Regan's gun into his belt with his left hand and beckoned the man north with his own gun. Regan started to walk.

When the shot came, Willmore felt the wind of it past his right cheek. It must have gone near Regan too because the man ducked and cried out.

Willmore turned quickly, saw nothing and waited with his nerves screaming for the next gun-flash. It came from away to his right. His reaction was instantaneous. He would have fired even if he had been mortally hit. But he wasn't hit and he heard his bullet strike. In the moon-shadow of the house, he heard a man grunt and go down. He fired a second time at the sound, turned to Regan and saw that the man was running. He fired a third shot close over his head and Regan came to an abrupt halt. Willmore walked up to him and said: "Now we'll walk."

Regan walked.

It was a hundred yards to the chaparral and Willmore didn't take a step that didn't feel like his last. Any second he expected the pursuit to start behind him. As they reached the edge of the chaparral, he heard the troopers come boiling into the yard, men shouted orders. By the sounds of things, most of them were afoot, but there was some horses there and a couple of them were ridden around to the north of the house. He pushed Regan ahead of him.

When they had gone a hundred yards with the thorns and branches tearing at them, Willmore called a halt. He turned Regan to face him. The big man looked scared.

He don't know how scared he should act, Willmore thought, *the way I feel right now*.

"Regan," he said, "make up your mind to talk right off. I don't have any time to waste."

"I don't know what you're talking about," Regan said.

"I'm talking about Mrs. Craytham. I want to know where she's at."

"How should I know."

"You out of your head. The two boys're at my camp. Sent by you to tell me that she's taken."

Regan looked genuinely astonished.

Half Willmore's attention was on his back-trail, putting himself in the places of the men back there. One of them had been shot and now they were asked to hunt a man in the dark. A man who was noted for his skill with a gun and his willingness to use it.

Regan said: "They lied."

"They say you took her."

"I'd be crazy to do a thing like that. We Reeses don't make war on women."

"You make war on anybody you reckon can't hit back."

"Look, Willmore, I don't know anything about the woman."

There were horses coming this way, beating their path through the brush. Willmore said: "Get into cover."

They edged their way into a thicket.

Willmore said: "Kneel down." Regan obeyed him. Willmore stood behind him with the muzzle of his gun at the back of the man's head. "Be still or I'll blow your brains out."

Regan didn't move.

The horsemen crashed by twenty yards to the east and went on. Willmore could hear them calling to each other. They were nervous.

Willmore got Regan on his feet and headed him west this time, circling him toward the horses. The man stumbled a lot and several times tried to tell Willmore that he knew nothing about Mrs. Craytham and this whole thing was crazy, but Willmore pushed him on.

They heard no more of the pursuit and Willmore knew that Morgan was no fool and had probably called it off till dawn when he would use his Waco tracker. They reached the horses without incident and Willmore told Regan to mount the roan. He had hoped that it would be Mrs. Craytham he would be taking away from here.

He rode due south now into the broken country where he would later have a chance to hide his tracks. He kept on the move until dawn and then halted in a rock-strewn arroyo. Wearily he and his prisoner stepped down from their horses.

In the cold light of dawn Regan looked terrible. His long blond hair was damp and stuck to his face with sweat when he took off his hat. His cheeks and eyes were puffed. His eyes flicked onto Willmore and away as though he couldn't bear the sight of him.

"Well," Willmore said when he had loosened the cinches of the horses, "do you talk?"

"For Christ sake," Regan said, "I told you and I told you. I don't know what you want to know."

"You're goin' to tell me just the same. Either I have Mrs. Craytham by tonight or you're goin' to be fit for the crows."

"You can't make me talk."

"Believe me, Regan, I could make a horse talk. I learned enough from the Comanches for that."

Cold fear showed in Regan's eyes.

"Willmore, I swear I don't know anything about the woman."

Willmore took off his gun-belt and laid the two guns side by side on a rock.

"I'm goin' to try beatin' it out of you,"

he said quietly. "An' if that don't work we'll try somethin' fancy an' Indian." He jerked his head toward the guns. "Try to get one of those."

Regan moved faster than he had thought possible. Stooping, he grasped a stone in each hand and ran in on Willmore, hurling the one in his right hand. As Willmore ducked under it, he grasped Willmore by the vest and smashed the rock in his left hand into his face.

Willmore went down, stunned.

He felt a boot crash into his rib-cage. He tried to grasp the boot and missed. He came up out of the dust as Regan ran for the guns. In that moment, Willmore didn't know whether he reached them or not. He took off in a flying tackle, managed to grasp the man's ankles and brought him down. At once Willmore leapt to his feet, saw the gun in the man's hand and leapt at him with both feet first. Bootheels landed in the man's belly. The wind went out of him with a sound like an organ. Willmore stumbled off him and stamped on the gun-wrist.

Regan shrieked.

Willmore kicked the gun away and said: "Get up, you yellow-bellied son-of-a-bitch."

Slowly Regan got to his feet, chest heaving, face misshapen with rage and pain.

Through his clenched teeth, he said almost sobbing: "I'm goin' to kill you. They were right. You're nothing but a trashy Indian. I'm going to kill you with my own hands."

Willmore smiled.

"You're alone now, baby-boy," he said. "You don't have the whole clan backin' you."

Regan charged.

Willmore sidestepped him, hit him in the belly and brought his knee up under his chin. That put the big man on his back, retching and shouting breathlessly and incoherently. He pulled himself over onto hands and knees and tried to get up.

"Want to talk?" Willmore asked.

"Screw you," Regan said or words to that effect. He got himself on knees alone and held his belly. He focused his eyes on the man above him and showed nothing but hate there. He got to his feet and Willmore hit him again. He went down and sounded like he was weeping. He stayed down a long time. Finally he sat up and glared at Willmore through his matted hair like an animal.

"I don't know," he said. "I don't know."

Willmore smiled.

"I have somethin'," he said, "that'll make you know."

Regan pushed the hair out of his eyes. "You can do what you like," he said. "You can only make me lie to you."

"No," Willmore said, "what I'm goin' to do only gets the truth. It's guaranteed."

He turned and walked to the dun, pulled the string on his saddle horn and took the rope down. Regan watched him. Willmore built a noose, swung it and tossed it over Regan's neck. The man made a feeble struggle to take it off, but Willmore strangled him down and laid him out flat on the ground. He turned him over with a toe. Regan started to fight to get his feet and Willmore pushed his face into the sand with a boot sole. Taking one of his hands he wrenched it behind his back and quickly bound it. The fight for freedom really began then. The man's efforts became frantic, so Willmore balled his fist and hit him hard behind the ear. After that it was no trouble at all to bind him hand and foot. Willmore rolled him over onto his back. Then he gathered greasewood and made his fire. By the time the flame was good and hot, Regan was awake. The man sat up and watched Willmore walk once more to his horse and take a running iron from the saddle.

Willmore came back to the fire, pulled on his gloves and put the iron in the fire.

He turned and looked at Regan.

"You Indian," Regan said. "You God-damned Indian."

Willmore allowed the iron to become

really hot before he took it from the fire.
Even the cooler end of the iron was hot
through the glove. The other end glowed
red-hot.

He walked toward Regan and the man
started crawling backward away from
him.

"You goin' to make me do it?"
Willmore asked.

Regan stopped crawling.

"You couldn't," he said. "A white man
couldn't."

He started crawling again as Willmore
leaned close. He stopped when the man
holding the glowing iron caught him by
the shirt and held him.

"Taste it," Willmore said through his
teeth and held the iron close to Regan's
face. The man shuddered back till his
head was pressed hard against the
ground, flinching away from the hot iron.

He looked up and his eyes met those of
the man above. He knew that this man
would brand him like an animal if he
didn't talk. All the success in the world
for the Reeses was not worth the pain.

"I'll talk," he said.

Willmore didn't move the iron.

"Talk," he said.

"Take the iron away first."

"Talk."

Regan said: "She's at the Starnholt's old place. Morgan's using it as a line camp."

Willmore seemed to relax. He stood up and stretched. The moment of tension had strained him.

"I hope you're tellin' the truth," he said.

He tossed the running iron into the sand and took a peggin string from a pocket. With this he bound Regan's legs. Then he took the rope off. There was puzzlement in Regan's eyes.

Willmore explained.

"It'll take you a little time to untie your ankles while I ride on."

"My God," Regan said, "you're not going to leave me here without a horse."

"That's what I'm going to do."

He walked away and put the fire out with handfuls of sand. He tested the running iron to check that it was cool and fastened it onto the saddle. He mounted and Regan started babbling, begging not to be left. A man afoot in this country was sentenced to death. Willmore knew that in this case that wasn't true. The pursuit would find him. That would be too soon for Willmore. Without another glance at Regan he rode out of the arroyo.

22

CHANGING horses to keep them fresh as he could, Willmore cut across country into the north-east, a trail that would take him past or close to the Reese place. That was a risk he had to take. There was no point in him covering his trail. The pursuit would come up with Regan and they would know exactly which way he had gone.

He rode hard, getting the utmost from his animals. Stopping only once for water when he came on it by chance, the exhaustion starting to tell on him. Happily the pace was such that he could not sleep in the saddle. He knew that he would have to have sleep soon or he would collapse, but he would have to keep going till he had Helen out of the Reeses' hands.

He passed within a mile of the Reese house by noon and the horses were starting to show signs of tiring. His only comfort was that the Reese horses and the troopers would also be tired. But they had the chance to remount at the house. Once he could get Helen back at his own camp, there might be a chance of safety for her. He bet that the army would not stand by and see a woman harmed. His one hope was that the army were now thoroughly in this chase and that the officer would be present if the Reeses came up with Helen.

He came to the Starnholt place an hour before dusk.

It was a small house, standing with a corral beneath a ridge. It was badly run down now. The Reeses had bought the owner out the year before using his war poverty as the lever.

His instinct bade him leave the horses in cover while he Indianed up to the place afoot. But time would not allow it. He had to have Helen out of there and on the trail quickly.

He lowered his pace to a steady lope and rode up to the house. He was within two hundred yards of the place when a man ran out into the yard and stood staring at him. At that distance he was not recognizable, but Willmore did not think that it was a Reese.

The man shouted something.

As the distance between Willmore and the house rapidly lessened, a second man ran out of the house. He stood irresolute for a moment, ran back to the building and appeared a moment later with a rifle in his hands.

Willmore, who was riding the dun, let the lead-rope of the roan go, yanked his gun from leather and as he came within range fired at the first man as he reached for his own weapon. Willmore missed and the man fired back. Willmore swerved his horse, dropped to the far side of it and fired once under the animal's neck. The man was knocked backward, tripped on his own heels and went down.

Willmore turned the horse again and swung up into the saddle as the rifle slammed.

The dun halted and went down as if it had run into a brickwall. Willmore kicked his feet free of the stirrup-irons and landed on his feet, running. The rifle slammed again, the man firing too hurriedly. Willmore's hat was whisked from his head and he flung himself flat on the ground, throwing his gun hand out in front of him.

He lined up on the man, cocked and fired as soon as he hit. The man yelled and dropped his rifle, his left arm hanging uselessly. As his right hand touched the butt of his revolver, Willmore fired again.

The heavy ball took the man in the chest and ran him backward against the wall of the house. He made a coughing sound and went down.

Willmore climbed to his feet and stood, eyes everywhere while he reloaded. That done, and seeing no further sign of movement, he went into the house. At first his eyes were blinded in the dim interior after the bright sunlight, but a small cry from one corner of the almost bare shack brought him to Helen Craytham.

She was lying on the dirt floor, bound hand and foot.

He put his gun away and drew his clasp-knife. Opening it he cut her bonds.

With his arms around her, she wept. She looked terrible. Her clothes were torn, her hair all over the place and her face dirty.

He kissed her and said: "There's no time for cryin', honey. We have to get out of here."

He helped her to her feet and her limbs were so cramped from being bound for so long that she cried out with the pain. He half carried her to a bunk and sat her on it.

"Get your circulation goin'," he told her, "While I catch up their horses."

She gave him a wan smile and he left her, going into the corral and using the rope from the dead dun, catching two of the three ponies that were there. They were no great shakes as horses, but at least they were fresh. He took the saddles from the dead horse and the roan and saddled the new ponies, then went back into the house for the woman. She was on her feet now trying to walk. He lifted her and carried her out and put her aboard a bay.

She said: "I knew you'd come, Tom."

He patted her arm and swung up on the other horse.

"We're goin' to ride," he said. "I have to get you to our camp. Can you stay astride?"

She nodded.

They rode.

The Waco Indian found Regan within a mile of where Willmore had left him three hours or more after the start of Willmore's wild ride north. By this time Regan was shouting like a madman and seemed to think the body of horsemen were wild Comanches come to get him.

Morgan ordered him to be carried into the shade and then when the brush was found to provide little, ordered a tarp stretched to shelter him from the burning sun.

He babbled as Morgan stood staring down at him.

"What's evident is that Willmore took him," he said.

Loge said: "What're we standing here for? He made Regan talk. He knows where the woman is and he's gone for her."

Morgan looked over his shoulder at the army officer and his half-dozen men gathered in a group about twenty yards off.

"We have to play this careful, Loge. The lieutenant catches sight of the woman and we're in a difficult spot."

Bull asked: "How do we play it then? By God, we have to catch up with Willmore."

"We will," Morgan said. "Now let's think. When Willmore sets the woman free, where will he go?"

"Back to his camp," Loge said.

"Precisely. Then it would be best if the lieutenant were there to catch him. Either that or on his route to cut him off. So we go after Willmore direct and if we get both him and the woman our luck's in. If we don't get him and the woman, the army gets at least him. Loge, you go with the army to identify him. Bull, send one of the Mexicans into town and get the sheriff to come out to Willmore's camp. We'll have him all ways."

"Christ," Bull said, "we don't want Charlie in on this."

"There's the matter of the cows," Morgan said with a smile. "They're branded Flying W and the owner is an outlaw."

They both looked at him and grinned.

Morgan ended: "Looks like Rege's coming around. Get him on a horse and have one of the men take him home. I'll go and talk to Lieutenant Garfield now."

As he walked off, they looked after him. There was self-satisfaction in every line of him.

There was little time to talk on that ride. Most of the time, they rode with Willmore in the lead with his eyes sharp for danger. When they came to the open prairies, however, they rode knee to knee. Once they stopped to water the horses and then there was time for her to come briefly into his arms. They kissed and Willmore knew that at last he had found the right woman. There was little said between them during the hurried flight through the brush, it was a hot business and they were occupied with their horses, their minds full of their danger for themselves and each other, but it brought them closer together. Somehow their lives had met fully and they knew that from now on they were shared.

Night dropped on them suddenly as it does in the brasada and they slowed their pace, but Willmore would not stop. He kept the horses at a hammering trot that saved the horses and made the riders suffer. Once around midnight he called a halt and off-saddled to allow the animals to roll. They were in need of water, but there was none. When they resaddled, they changed horses to give themselves a change of pace and the animals a change of rider. Riders and horses were refreshed. By now Willmore rode in a dream of tiredness. The woman bore up well.

When he asked her if she could stand the pace, she said simply: "If you can keep on going, I can."

Two hours from dawn, the horses showed signs of not being able to hold up much longer, so Willmore halted again. This time they were lucky enough to be near water. Animals and riders drank. Willmore picketed the horses on the sparse grass while he and Helen caught a brief sleep. They dropped off dead in each others' arms.

At dawn, Willmore was brought wide awake by one of the animals nickering. He was on his feet at once. He could not see what had alarmed the animal, but he at once saddled both animals and got the woman astride.

He never did find out what made the horse nicker, but he took it as fair warning and they got on their way. The animals were still tired and he could get out of them no more than a shuffling trot.

When he reckoned they were within five miles of the cow-camp and as he thought on Cary range, he again halted.

Dismounting, he pulled a piece of paper from his pocket and using the saddle as a support wrote with a stub of pencil. When he had finished he folded the paper and handed it to Helen.

"Give that to Bill Cary first thing," he said.

She tucked it down the neck of her dress between her breasts.

"Do you mean me to go ahead?" she asked.

"Yes."

"I'd rather you stayed with me."

"You'll see me soon enough," he said. "Right now it's best for everybody if I stay away from the herd. Remember, in Texas I'm an outlaw."

"I'll do it," she said, "but I don't like it."

She leaned from the saddle and kissed him on the mouth. He held her face in his hand and smiled up at her.

"There never was a woman like you," he said.

When the shot came, it was so close

that he heard the shrill whine of it just over their heads.

Willmore turned quickly.

Not a hundred yards away, coming through a break in the chaparral was a horseman with a smoking rifle in his hands.

Willmore lashed Helen's horse with his quirt and bellowed: "Ride."

The animal bunched its hind legs and jumped. Willmore bounded into his own saddle, spurred savagely after Helen and lashed her animal again as it refused to hit a gallop. This time the animal ran, tired as it was. Willmore took the quirt from his wrist leaned across to Helen's racing pony and shouted: "Use it. Go ahead."

She took the whip from him and used it.

Willmore looked back and saw the riders come boiling out of the brush. He counted six of them and heaved his Remington carbine from its sheath. Before he could let off more than a couple of shots, they hit the brush again and lost them to view. They were on a trail.

Willmore yelled: "Follow the trail."

Helen turned a scared face to him and he heard her shrill: "Stay with me."

"Go ahead," he yelled back, pulled his mount back onto its haunches and opened fire along the trail as the first rider came into sight. The horse went down, throwing the man clear. He pumped another round into the breech and fired again as a second and third rider came into sight.

He hit neither, deliberately turned his horse and plunged into what seemed not such thick brush to the right of the trail. He knew that it was him they wanted, not Helen.

He hadn't covered a hundred yards when he heard their crashing pursuit and their shouts. He used steel on the pony, but it had given its best and could give him no more. By the sounds behind him he knew that the men after him were better mounted. It didn't seem possible that he would find a place to fort up in around here, but that was what he wanted if he stayed alive even a little longer. He prayed fervently that he had decoyed them away from Helen.

Then suddenly it happened.

The brush stopped abruptly and the pony he was on nearly pitched head first into an arroyo. He swung it to the right and ran along the rim of the dried watercourse. He covered a hundred yards and saw the rocks away to his right which would make him circle and come nearly back on his pursuers. But it was shelter and that was what he wanted. He turned right again.

Almost at once two riders burst from cover and headed for him at right angles to his line of travel. Even above the thud of his horse's hoofs he heard the sharp crack of the rifles.

He hit the grade up into the rocks and the pony, tired beyond endurance, nearly floundered. Sheer horsemanship kept it on its feet and it heaved and panted to the top of the slope. He rode it clear into the rocks, slipped from the saddle and flung himself down.

There were four men in sight now. Two within a hundred yards and two more further off. Even as he sighted on the first man, several more riders came into view.

He fired and took the man in the lead clean out of the saddle, dumping him out of sight at the feet of his horse.

The ground was rough here and without pause every man out there pulled up and got out of the saddle, hugging dirt as any sensible man would do.

He fired at the crown of a hat and lifted it from its owner's head.

Silence took over the scene.

Willmore started stuffing fresh rounds into the magazine of the Remington. He had to be sparing with them and every shot would have to tell. This was going to be a delaying game. He would get out of here after dark and then it wouldn't be easy.

23

THE girl realized suddenly that Willmore was no longer with her. Fear shot through her, paralyzing her for a frightening moment. She heard shooting and even with her fear she nearly turned back so that she could be with Willmore.

But she knew that she could do no good and went on. The animal slowed and she used Willmore's quirt again.

The trail was easy to follow. It wound to right and left, but it was well used and she had no difficulty in staying on it.

After five minutes' riding she came to an open prairie and started across it.

A shout and she glanced off to the left and saw a line of horsemen going in the same direction as herself.

A man broke from them and came toward her. She had time only to see that they were all dressed in blue and that most of them had black faces and she fled on.

She did not look back until she had crossed the prairie and was about to plunge into the brush again. When she looked she saw that there were a half-dozen cavalry men and they were streaming after her. She didn't know what to do, but she remembered that all Willmore had said that she would not be safe till she reached Bill Cary at the cow-camp. She kept on.

Another five minutes along this new trail and she came on a man mounted on a claybank horse with a big roan steer on the end of a rope. He looked up in some astonishment as she thundered toward him. There was only time to see that it was one of the Chavez boys before she was past.

Then suddenly the brush stopped again and she was in the open, out of the oven-like heat and there before her was a wide corral full of bawling cattle. There perched on a rail-fence was a man, shouting. Beyond him were other men, some mounted, some on foot.

She rode along the edge of the corral and was among them. Her horse stopped, with splayed legs and hanging head.

She fell rather than slipped from the saddle and strong hands gripped her. She turned and saw a bearded face near hers.

"Bill Cary," she said hoarsely. She didn't know it, but she shouted.

The man grinned a little and said: "In person."

Straightway, she remembered the note that Willmore had given her. The pounding of hoofs was approaching. She looked up to see the soldiers with two white men in their lead cantering toward them. She took the note from her bosom and thrust it into Bill Cary's hands.

"Read it, quick," she whispered.

"He opened it and read it.

He gave her a brief grin, thrust the paper into his pants' pocket and quickly spoke to the man next to him. This man turned to the next. A third, when he heard, wheeled his horse and rode headlong for the wagon where he awoke several men sleeping there. They straightway leapt to their feet, saddled their horses and rode for the branding chute.

The cavalry halted in a cloud of dust. The young officer and the white civilian came forward.

"We're looking for Thomas Willmore," the white civilian began.

The officer touched his arm.

"If you don't mind, sir," he said, "I'll handle this."

Loge Reese said gruffly: "As you wish. Go ahead."

The soldier halted his horse and said: "Who's in charge here?" He looked what he was, a boy tackling a man's job and doing the best he could with the problem.

"I am, son," Bill Cary said.

The boy flushed. He hoped his men hadn't heard that.

"I'm looking for Tom Willmore. He's wanted for murder and armed robbery.

Bill Cary looked at the young man earnestly. "I'll be straight with you, mister. Willmore *was* here. But he rid off."

"Where did he go?"

"Don't rightly know. But I know what he aimed to do."

"What was that?"

"He went skunk shootin'."

The young man looked surprised. He glanced around at the tanned faces around him, Anglo and Mexican. There was no glimmer of a smile there.

"Skunk shooting?"

"Yeah. He reckoned the stink of Reeses in this country was somethin' awful an' as a patriotic citizen he should ought to do somethin' about it."

The young man's flush disappeared and he went white to the mouth with anger.

"I'll thank you not to fool with me, sir," he shouted. "This is a matter of life and death. This Willmore is riding around the country like a crazyman. Nobody's safe from him."

Helen said: "I just spent a day with him. He didn't harm me any. In fact, he saved my life."

The lieutenant seemed to see her for the first time.

"Are you the lady who just rode away from us, ma'am." She nodded. "May I ask how you came to spend a day in the murderer's company?"

"You may. I was taken prisoner by the Reeses and he got me away."

Loge showed immense astonishment.

"That's a fantastic lie," he said with quiet conviction.

Five cowmen at once unlimbered their guns. The officer and the Reese were completely covered.

Bill Cary said: "Swallow that, Loge, or I'll knock it down your throat with your teeth."

When Loge looked like he would give a furious reply, the lieutenant said: "You would be advised to do so, Mr. Reese. These men have the advantage."

The men from the wagon came riding up. When they saw the state of affairs here, they also drew their guns.

The officer said: "Do you think it's wise to draw weapons on the army?"

Cary laughed.

"Bless your heart, man," he said. "We ain't drawin' on the army. Just this Reese here."

The lieutenant would have said something more, but he was interrupted by the sound of drumming hoofs. The young man and Loge Reese turned their heads and saw Morgan and Henry riding hard toward them. They halted in a swirl of dust and took the scene in.

"What goes on here, young man?" Morgan demanded of the officer.

Lieutenant said: "Put up your guns, men, all I want here is Thomas Willmore."

"I didn't hear that coyote take back what he said about the lady."

Loge said to Morgan: "This woman accused us of taking her prisoner."

Morgan said to the officer: "That is a preposterous suggestion. But we have more important things to talk about. Tom Willmore is not the only thing you have come here about. There's the cattle."

"What cattle?" The soldier looked surprised.

"These." Morgan threw a hand toward the scattered herd and to the cattle held in the pen. "They belong to a man who is an outlaw. The sheriff is now on his way to impound them. You should hold them for him. These men must stop branding at once."

Bill Cary did an astonishing thing. He said: "Put your guns away men. You won't need them."

The men looked at him doubtfully, but, as he put his own weapon away, they followed suit.

The officer said to him: "Is that right? Are these Willmore's cattle?"

"They are not," Cary said.

Morgan shouted: "He lies. Look at the brand."

There was a silence. Loge turned himself in the saddle and looked at the cow in the chute near him. The Mexican sitting on the chute rail was grinning. Loge stiffened and looked beyond into the holding pen now crowded with cattle

288

branded that day. What he saw flabbergasted him.

He gasped: "They ain't branded with the Flying W."

Morgan exclaimed and moved his horse for a better look. He saw a Box C on the animals' flanks. He looked at Bill Cary, then Helen.

"What kind of a trick is this?" he demanded.

Bill Cary looked innocent.

"Trick," he said. "This ain't no trick. We're brandin' for the owner."

"But the Box C is the Craytham brand."

"That's right. Mrs. Craytham is the owner."

Morgan looked stricken.

"This isn't possible," was all he managed to gasp.

The officer asked Helen: "Is this so, ma'am? Are these your cattle?"

"They most certainly are."

The lieutenant turned to Morgan.

"It looks like we don't have any more business here, sir. I suggest we go."

Furiously, Morgan said: "But we have business just up the road. My boys have Willmore cornered. Come on."

He turned and rode off to the north. Loge and the officer wheeled their animals and pelted after him. The whole army patrol turned on itself and cantered off after them.

Helen Craytham was pale. She turned to Bill Cary.

"We must do something," she said. "They'll kill him. He led them away from me. We have to do something."

Cary said: "Tom told me to do nothing. We turn on the army and we lose the cows."

"What're a bunch of cows to a man's life?"

"The future for a whole lot of folks. We can't go undoin' everythin' Tom did."

Mose Green came forward.

"You ain't gonna miss one lil ole nigger, Tom," he said.

Bill said: "There's nothin' you can do, Mose."

290

Green smiled a little and said: "You just watch me." He rode away slowly after the departing riders, not hurrying.

24

THERE was time to think up there in the rocks. The heat from the sun was enough to addle a man's brains. It burned his eyes as it reflected from the rocks. Water was his main problem. He had half a canteen on the horse and it was warm and brackish already.

But the sun had started to sink and he knew that if he could hold out for another hour or so there was a chance of getting away under cover of darkness. A slim chance, but the only chance that would come to him.

For the last hour it seemed that his attackers were content to wait it out as he was, but now with the approaching of darkness, they began to show urgency. He had seen Morgan and the soldiers ride up and knew that the real ball would now start. The sight of the soldiers put him in a real fix. He had no wish to start trouble with them for a shot soldier would make it a federal affair. As he saw them scattering out around him, he knew that any minute now he would be a fugitive from something more than the county law.

Lying there, there had been time to think. He knew that the Reeses dare not stop till they had him dead. He knew too much about them. With the return of his memory, they were indicted in mind. He knew that Morgan Reese was masquerading in this country under a false name as were the whole of his clan. John Morgan was his real name and he had gained his working capital by depredations up in Kansas and Missouri. He had found safety with all the cleverness which came naturally to him by hiding in the midst of his late enemies in Texas. A friend of the governor, he had been safe there. Safe till he had been recognized by the former Rebel soldier, Tom Willmore and his brother Bart. Bart was dead and Morgan would not be safe till Tom was dead.

Willmore licked his dry lips and spied a soldier creeping in from rock to rock over to his right. Problem: how to stop the man without killing or wounding him.

Suddenly, the mood of the attackers changed. Dark would be here soon and they had to have him before it cloaked his movements. They starting bearing down on him with rifle fire.

The horse was the first to be hit.

It went down screaming and he had to turn and shoot it through the head with his revolver. The flies arrived as the blood spilled and the place seemed alive with them. To add to his difficulties a bullet went through the canteen and spilled his precious water.

My God, he thought in despair, *I'm a dead duck*.

The air was filled with flying lead. It forced his head down and while it was there he heard the sounds of the men running in on him. Feet pounded on hard ground and the accoutrement of cavalrymen rattled.

He glimpsed a man in civilian clothes

dodging from brush to rock and snapped a shot at him, saw him go down and heard his yell of alarm and pain. He reckoned with the army there, there must be upward of twenty men around him. The odds weren't good. The nearest man was within thirty yards of him.

Then suddenly out of the distant brush more horsemen appeared and he guessed that it was the sheriff and a posse. The odds were mounting.

The movement of the sun seemed to have slowed. In despair he watched the sky and counted out his ammunition. Two more full loads for the rifle and two for the pistol.

He fired at a hat and missed.

A cavalryman ran into the open, his black face working with excitement. Willmore aimed with great care and shot him in the leg.

That stopped them for a few seconds.

Flies settled on his face and he brushed them away irritably.

Back at the herd Jed Cary headed off an

irate cow that had come to rescue its calf as the little creature went into the chute for its brand and joined his brother Bill.

"Bill," he said, "our old man's dead an' the Reeses did it. It ain't proper us Carys to nurse cows while Tom does the fightin'."

Bill nodded.

"I'm thinkin' the same thing," he said.

Jed said: "Sam an' me'll ride then."

"Watch out for yourselves."

"We'll do that."

Jed rode over to his brother who was watching the outskirts of the main herd to the west.

"Let's go," he said.

The two Carys turned their horses and rode north. Miguel Chavez watched them go and nodded to his brother, Chico. This squat Mexican grinned briefly and followed the Carys.

Darkness came suddenly and they gave him no chance. He had checked his guns by touch and was preparing to creep through the rocks northward when they came running in on him. They did not make the mistake of coming from all sides and running the risk of being hit by their own shooting, but attacked from the south.

He did not hear them till they hit the bottom of the grade and then it was too late to run.

He threw himself down, saw a line of shadowy forms and opened fire.

He never knew if he had made a hit. The fire they returned was so withering that he knew that the knoll was no longer tenable.

Crawling to the other side of the small hill, he peered out of the rocks and saw nothing but rocks and brush beneath him. Behind him he could hear the men climbing at a scrambling run. He could turn and fight, maybe kill two or three, but after that it was finish. He thought of Helen and the future.

He got to his feet and, crouched down, started at a scrambling run down the rocks, expecting a shot from the rear at any second.

He was halfway down when he heard a shout from behind.

"He ain't here, Morg. He musta come your way."

Booted feet scrabbled rock above him. Nobody started down after him. That meant there were others down there waiting for him. He eased off to the left, going with tremendous caution, rifle held ready for a hurried shot.

He covered twenty or thirty feet in dead silence and met no one. Maybe his hunch was right and this side was unguarded.

In the next second, he almost trod on a man. Suddenly a heavy shape rose out of the murk.

"Who the hell—?" the man said.

Quickly, Willmore swung the butt of the rifle. He aimed badly in the darkness and did no more than clip the fellow's shoulder. There was a curse and a shout followed by a shot that came so close that he felt the burn of the bullet past his cheek. Flight could mean death now, so

Willmore took the only action open to him. He charged.

The two men met head on, clubbing and cursing. The crown of Willmore's hat was crushed against his skull by the barrel of a pistol and he stumbled to his knees. He struck out in a blind sweep with the rifle and must have caught his adversary's legs. The man yelled and stumbled, walking into Willmore and going over. Willmore rose and swung the rifle downward viciously, struck rock and lost the weapon as the man came back in a rushing charge.

Willmore used his heel on the uncertain shape and stopped the rush. The man went down and Willmore tried to turn and flee, but a hand gripped his ankle and he was hurled to the ground with breath-robbing force. He rolled and came to his knees, sucking breath into his starved lungs, his right hand fumbling for the gun he had taken from Regan. He drew it and fired as the other man reared to his feet. There was an answering shot that ripped at Willmore's sleeve and then he fired direct into the muzzle-flame. The man went over without a sand.

Willmore turned and ran, got caught in brush and fought his way out of it.

Somewhere above him a man yelled: "He's comin' your way, Loge."

A rifle slammed flatly, but no lead came near Willmore. He forced ahead, stumbling noisily over rocks and getting entangled in brush.

The rifle was fired again and this time the lead came close. Willmore reckoned he was running into a line of men waiting for him.

He turned south, hoping to outflank the party that had first charged him. There could be safety in risk.

From behind him a voice bawled: "Comin' south."

He stopped abruptly and lay down, trying to recover his breath and thinking.

There was a short silence and then men began shouting their opinions as to where he might be.

Morgan's voice came.

"He's to the west of the hill. Loge, spread your men out. I'll comb the hill."

Loge's voice came back.

"Leave him till light. We lost enough men."

"We get him now," Morgan roared back. "Come light he'll be gone."

There came the sound of men beating their way through rocks and brush. Willmore glimpsed a hat against the somber night sky not ten yards from him and snapped a shot at it. He heard the man throw himself into cover and yell that the son-of-a-bitch was over here.

Morgan started yelling: "Give yourself up, Willmore, you don't stand a snowball's chance in hell."

Willmore fired at the voice and started working his way south.

His eyes were becoming used to the dark now. There were some stars and they helped a mite. The knoll reared up dark to his left and he could see men moving about to his right. They started to close in on him and he knew the only chance he stood was to rush them and shoot his way though them. The odds would be heavily against him, but they were the only odds offered.

He was about to jump to his feet and start his charge when he heard the rumble of hoofs.

At once his horseman's mind estimated numbers and their distance away from him. At least twenty animals at about a quarter-mile.

Other ears had heard too.

There were shouts in the darkness all around him and he knew that those horses belonged to the men searching for him. Somebody had stampeded them. Hope rose in Willmore. Men started running and shouting. Morgan's voice rose in anger, telling them to stay where they were, they could catch the animals when it was light. They were here to get Willmore now.

Willmore started his charge, but at the last moment, he changed his mind as to his manner. He got to his feet and started walking steadily toward the spot from whence Morgan's voice had come.

The horses were coming this way. A lot of shrill yelling came to him on the night air and as he walked he tried to analyze the sound he heard. He reckoned that the saddle-horses were being chased by riders.

The damned fools, he thought. *I told Bill to stay with the herd. Now we're all ruined.*

The loose horses swept across the open space. He heard Morgan's men out there yelling and trying to catch them. Then there was gunfire and a pandemonium of yells and shots. The horses swept by the east side of the knoll away from Willmore and crashed on into the brush. The shooting continued. He glimpsed dim forms of horsemen and saw the bright stab of muzzle-flash. The riders crashed through the rocks, firing and shouting, then, as quickly as they had come, were gone.

There was a man in front of Willmore.

"Who's this?" the man demanded. His voice was Morgan's.

Willmore said: "This is Willmore," and

felt rather than saw the man's gun-hand come up.

They pressed their triggers together, only Morgan's gun was loaded and Willmore's was empty. The hammer fell with a click on the empty chamber. For a moment, panic flushed through him. He hurled the gun with all his might at the figure ahead of him and threw himself to one side.

As he hit dirt, he heard the man cry out. Morgan's gun fired again.

Dust was blown into Willmore's face. He choked on it and heaved his own Remington from leather, cocking and firing in one movement.

The dark shape that was Morgan seemed to be lifted momentarily from its feet and then thrown loosely to the ground.

Willmore heaved himself to his feet and started running north in the direction the riders had taken. A knot of men appeared suddenly from the gloom, hurrying in his direction. He was going too fast to stop.

Before they had time to do anything about him, he was on them, shouting and firing.

A man went down, clutching desperately at the man beside him. Willmore's shoulder took another in the chest and sent him into these two and then Willmore was past, running as fast as his cowman's boots would allow.

Somebody fired after him, but the shot went a couple of feet wide to the right. He ran on until he could run no more. Gasping for breath he stopped and started reloading his gun. He swore he would never be caught again with an empty gun in his life.

The hoofs of a horse padded on hard ground.

He turned, raising his gun. There was a rider against dark brush twenty yards off.

"Sing out or I shoot," he said.

The man said: "Patron, it is I, Chico."

Willmore dragged his leaden feet forward. Chico slipped from the saddle. Willmore was so overcome that he briefly put an arm around the Mexican's shoulder.

"*Dios,*" he said in Spanish, "I was never more glad to see a man in my life."

Chico laughed his pleasure.

"Me also, patron. We thought you dead. Quick, mount my horse and I will get up behind. It is better that we are a long way from here I think."

"Have you others with you?"

"They are ahead. I came back to scout. Come, hurry."

Willmore forked the horse. Chico vaulted up behind him and they rode north. Inside a half-mile other shadowy riders were on the trail. Jed and Sam Cary were there with Mose Green, crowding around to shake his hand. There was a lot of soft relieved laughter in the dark.

"Where's Bill and the rest?" Willmore asked.

Mose Green answered:

"They's with the cows like you said, boy. We'm the bad ones. We'm all outlaws together now. Bill Cary, he got it all in your note."

"Yeah," Jed said. "Us Cary boys and Chico here reckoned you wasn't the only one owed the Reeses somethin'. Mose just natcherly come along. An' here we are."

Willmore smiled in the darkness.

"Well, I'm damned glad to hear you boys decided to break the law."

Mose Green came forward with a spare horse, ready saddled. Willmore thanked him and mounted. As the moon rose, they hurried north. Willmore thought about Helen and the two boys, his ready-made family. He wanted like hell to see her but he knew that wasn't possible, not yet. He would be able to think about their meeting as he rode. He looked into the future and reckoned that for the first time in many a day it looked pretty good. Bill Cary and the rest would be able to move the herd north, there were enough of them now. The cows were safe with Helen's brand on them. They would drive to Doan's Crossing and then leave Texas for the Indian Nations.

There Willmore would be waiting for her and their shared future.

He began to hum softly to himself in time to the steady beat of the trotting horse. Life was good.

THE END

SUNDANCE: SILENT ENEMY
by John Benteen

Both the Indians and the U.S. Cavalry were being victimized. A lone crazed Cheyenne was on a personal war path against both sides. They needed to pit one man against one crazed Indian. That man was Sundance.

LASSITER
by Jack Slade

Lassiter wasn't the kind of man to listen to reason. Cross him once and he'd hold a grudge for years to come—if he let you live that long. But he was no crueler than the men he had killed, and he had never killed a man who didn't need killing.

LAST STAGE TO GOMORRAH
by Barry Cord

Jeff Carter, tough ex-riverboat gambler, now had himself a horse ranch that kept him free from gunfights and card games. Until Sturvesant of Wells Fargo showed up. Jeff owed him a favour and Sturvesant wanted it paid up. All he had to do was to go to Gomorrah and recover a quarter of a million dollars stolen from a stagecoach!

McALLISTER ON THE COMANCHE CROSSING
by Matt Chisholm

The Comanche, deadly warriors and the finest horsemen in the world, reckon McAllister owes them a life—and the trail is soaked with the blood of the men who had tried to outrun them before.

QUICK-TRIGGER COUNTRY
by Clem Colt

Turkey Red hooked up with Curly Bill Graham's outlaw crew and soon made a name for himself. But wholesale murder was out of Turk's line, so when range war flared he bucked the whole border gang alone . . .

PISTOL LAW
by Paul Evan Lehman

Lance Jones came back to Mustang for just one thing—Revenge! Revenge on the people who had him thrown in jail; on the crooked marshal; on the human vulture who had already taken over the town. Now it was Lance's turn . . .

GUNSLINGER'S RANGE
by Jackson Cole

Three escaped convicts are out for revenge. They won't rest until they put a bullet through the head of the dirty snake who locked them behind bars.

RUSTLER'S TRAIL
by Lee Floren

Jim Carlin knew he would have to stand up and fight because he had staked his claim right in the middle of Big Ike Outland's best grass. Jim also had a score to settle with his renegade brother.

Larry and Stretch:
THE TRUTH ABOUT SNAKE RIDGE
by Marshall Grover

The troubleshooters came to San Cristobal to help the needy. For Larry and Stretch the turmoil began with a brawl, then an ambush, and then another attempt on their lives—all in one day.

WOLF DOG RANGE
by Lee Floren

Montana was big country, but not big enough for a ruthless land-grabber like Will Ardery. He would stop at nothing, unless something stopped him first—like a bullet from Pete Manly's gun.

Larry and Stretch: DEVIL'S DINERO
by Marshall Grover

Plagued by remorse, a rich old reprobate hired the Texas Troubleshooters to deliver a fortune in greenbacks to each of his victims. Even before Larry and Stretch rode out of Cheyenne, a traitor was selling the secret and the hunt was on.

CAMPAIGNING
by Jim Miller

Ambushed on the Santa Fe trail, Sean Callahan is saved from dying by two Indian strangers. Then the trio is joined by a former slave called Hannibal. But there'll be more lead and arrows flying before the band join the legendary Kit Carson in his campaign against the Comanches.

DONOVAN
by Elmer Kelton

Donovan was supposed to be dead. The town had buried him years before when Uncle Joe Vickers had fired off both barrels of a shotgun into the vicious outlaw's face as he was escaping from jail. Now Uncle Joe had been shot—in just the same way.

CODE OF THE GUN
by Gordon D. Shirreffs

MacLean came riding home with saddle-tramp written all over him, but sewn in his shirt-lining was an Arizona Ranger's star. MacLean had his own personal score to settle—in blood and violence!

GAMBLER'S GUN LUCK
by Brett Austen

Gamblers hands are clean and quick with cards, guns and women. But their names are black, and they seldom live long. Parker was a hell of a gambler. It was his life—or his death . . .